BLEED AWAY THE SKY

BRIAN FATAH STEELE

Cover Design © 2019 by Don Noble
https://roosterrepublicpress.com

ISBN-13: 978-1-947522-17-6
ISBN-10: 1-947522-17-5

BLOODSHOT BOOKS

READ UNTIL YOU BLEED!

DEDICATION

For my brother Adam.
Miss you, man...

ACKNOWLEDGEMENTS

I'll probably forget some names here, but know you're appreciated. Douglas A. Brookes was my beta-reader and proofed this book, likely allowing it to even get published. Daniel Weymouth, Brittany Amicone Weymouth, April McKinley, Eric and Courtney Cornell, Kendell Gibson, Sierra Jones, Joe Shaffer, Brianna Barker, Phoenix Huff, Jonathan and Annie Joyce, Ricky Harris, Jose Martinez, Staci Donnalley, and Dawne Lemery Bednarek. Thanks for all the support.

Pete Kahle made it possible for this story to be told, and I can't thank him enough. A number of other people in the industry have been incredibly kind. John Claude Smith, Taylor Grant, Erin Sweet-Al Mehairi, Robert S. Wilson, Anthony Rivera, Sharon Lawson, Salome Jones, Tristan Thorne, Matthew J. Leverton, Nate Southard, S.P. Miskowski, Michelle Garza, Laurel Stark, Ken Gordhamer, John McCallum Swain, Sara Lunsford, CL Stegall, and Court Ellen.

I have to thank the music of Lana Del Rey. This particular novel was written exclusively to her discography.

Mom and Dad, thanks for putting up with me. Nathan, Jordan, and Quintin, thanks for being awesome "little" brothers. The plushy Cthulhus I got the nephews is just the start.

Laken Anderson, thank you for being you. Always.

BLEED AWAY THE SKY

BRIAN FATAH STEELE

PROLOGUE

Mommy didn't bleed her own blood.

Audrey couldn't recall when she realized that. She wasn't even really sure what it meant, only that it was true. She lay in her bed, clutching her stuffed giraffe, and listened to the sounds coming from her Mommy's bedroom. They were scary sounds, as scary as Mommy could be sometimes.

They had ravioli for dinner that night and Audrey had been delighted. She'd had a good day at school, getting an A+ on her spelling test and winning the game of kickball during recess. She had been so excited by the ravioli, she didn't notice her Mommy's mood. Manic, anxious, fidgety. After eating, Audrey wanted to go out back and play in her sandbox but had gotten snapped at. It was too late to get all dirty.

Audrey, even at six years old, knew better. It was almost time for one of Mommy's alone times. The rest of dinner was finished in silence.

Audrey took a short bath that night without bubbles. She played with her duckies out of routine, but her heart wasn't in it. Mommy didn't stay in the bathroom, instead she was already getting things ready in her bedroom. A big girl now, Audrey got cleaned up all by herself, including washing her hair, and drying off. She loved her big fluffy unicorn towel and wished she could use it as a blanket.

That had been forever ago. Hours. Mommy had kissed her goodnight, barely paying attention, and tucked her into bed with a book. But as it always happened on nights like this, she said strange things to Audrey. Warned her not to leave her room unless she absolutely had to use the bathroom, not to knock on Mommy's door. Then she had said the stranger things, the stuff that Audrey never understood.

"Inside us blooms a feast for gods, dearest. As I flow, so shall you some day. It's a great honor! You'll understand when you're older."

Audrey wanted to understand now, but she knew better than to ask any more questions. Mommy got upset and her words didn't come out right. So instead, Audrey just nodded and let her Mommy leave. She ignored her book, clutched onto her giraffe, and waited for the sounds to begin.

Audrey was too young to understand that this happened two or three times a month, and that those sounds emanated from her mother's room for an average of twenty minutes. She only understood that her mother was tired the next day, often forgetful. Although Audrey never did quite piece together what her mother was doing, it was a day after one of those infamous alone times, exhausted and spacey, that her mother had crashed her car into the rear end of a tractor trailer. Audrey was only seven when it happened.

Her mother never got a chance to explain...

CHAPTER 1

Audrey Darrow scowled at the remains of her eggs and pushed the plate away. While the pancakes had been excellent, light and buttery, the yellow goop beside them tasted like something made from chemicals. She stretched her tan legs out beneath the booth—not a hard feat when you're only slightly above five foot tall—and sighed. Only two days into the road trip and she was already regretting it.

The Arizona heat was scorching in June, the sun baking the desert across the street from the diner. Miles upon miles of nothingness. Audrey understood the feeling. She had enjoyed the drive down, flying through the desolation. She found the open sky and barren landscape soothing.

Elliot had picked out this spot ahead of time. Some formerly famous motel attached to a down home eatery. Its renown must have been decades ago because it was in a sorry state now. She suspected Elliot knew that and had picked it because it was cheap. She could appreciate that.

Formica tables and pale green cushioned booths that had long ago lost any comfort, everything was chipped and worn down. The large windows had years' worth of finger prints and smears on them, an accumulation of grime. Their waitress had been pleasant enough, but looked like a caricature in her pink dress, white apron, and greying hair falling from its bun. The motel stretching out along the road had a fair number of vacancies, the two twin beds they had slept on likely not updated since sometime in the 70's. The orange and brown wallpaper alone was worthy of an acid trip. Audrey tried not to think about what she had shared the sheets with and had taken another shower when she woke.

There were going to be a lot more places like this, questionable spots in which to bed down and restaurants that barely deserved the title. A cross-country trip, from northern California to New York and back, in three weeks or so. It's what Elliot had wanted to do, and she reluctantly agreed. Mostly because he was paying for the bulk of it.

It wasn't like Audrey was abandoning a whole lot back home. She had a one-bedroom apartment, in a three-story walkup with perpetually leaky pipes, which sat in front of a rail line. A freelance web designer, she took work wherever she could find it. It was rarely artistic or engaging, her last gig for the pet shop down the street. She made just enough money to pay her bills, feed herself, and drown her sorrows all too often at the corner bar. One of the bartenders there had the hots for her, and while he was sweet enough, Audrey couldn't summon enough conviction to care. And despite what Elliot tried to say, no company was going to hire a web designer, regardless of her talent, with only a high school diploma.

She was depressed and knew it. She always had been. Initially, she thought the trip would be a sort of escape, a way to perhaps examine her life from the outside and gain a new perspective. Audrey knew she was good at what she did, all of it self-taught, but it didn't fill her with any sense of purpose. She had no sense of actually living life, just existing. All the research she had done on the subjects of depression and anxiety said that this feeling was common, but the few solutions given weren't options for her. Most cost money.

For some reason, Elliot wanted to spend his money and time on her.

He came back from the restroom, weaving between the booths. Elliot was two years younger than her at twenty-two, and he had just graduated from college with a degree in industrial engineering. Audrey understood precisely zero about his degree, but he seemed passionate about it. He was due to start a job at a major firm in July, once they had returned from the trip. He had received a ridiculous settlement from his father's death that he was using to bankroll their little adventure.

Their father's death. The father that she had never known.

"You're not going to eat those eggs?" he asked, eyeing her plate.

"All yours."

She couldn't help but smile as she watched him shovel the horrible tasting eggs into his mouth. Nothing seemed to faze him. She wished she had some of his easy-going nature. While they had some of the same facial features, and olive skin, that was where their similarities ended. Audrey was petite and blonde, easily labeled an introvert, while Elliot was tall with dark hair, and gregarious. His T-shirt had a picture of a dancing alligator on it.

Audrey was still getting used to the idea that she had a brother. He had appeared a little over a year ago, ready for hugs. She had spent three months just verifying he wasn't some psycho.

"You ready?" he asked, pulling out his wallet.

Audrey nodded, getting her purse. It was little more than a black canvas bag, but she carried her life in it. One of her little neuroses. Walking out of the diner, she shielded her eyes from the Arizona glare. The heat beat down on them as they walked over to their motel room. Audrey paused and stared out into the desert as Elliot fiddled with the lock. The emptiness looked inviting.

"Whatcha looking at?"

Audrey shrugged and followed him inside. The vomit-inducing colors danced on the walls. Audrey considered switching into flip flops but decided against it. They'd still be in the desert for a few more days, and there was no point in getting her feet dirty. As it was, she could already feel a thin layer of desert on her legs and arms. Tying her shoulder length hair back in a short ponytail, she packed up the last few things left around the room.

"So there's an alpaca farm nearby," said Elliot. "Wanna see some alpacas?"

"Are you serious?"

"I can't tell by your face if you're happy with the idea of seeing alpacas or not."

Audrey shook her head and laughed. "Sure, alpacas. Why the hell not?"

"Awesome! Let's get packed up."

Audrey carried her bag outside and put it in the trunk of Elliot's car. He stuck his in as well and then walked the room keys back to the manager's office while she waited. A truck drove past and honked at her, eliciting another smile. She was going to have to keep in good spirits for the trip, try not to let herself agonize over the life waiting for her back home. For Elliot, at least.

The desert, vast and bleak, offered up no answers.

CHAPTER 2

"**H**urry up," said Kristie.

Megan jiggled the door handle, scowling. "I'm going."

"Let's go," said Royce.

Royce grabbed Kristie's hand and pushed past, his sister Megan trailing behind him, as they entered the old building. It had been an opulent hotel once, back in the heyday of Eldridge, Ohio. They didn't care, it was just somewhere to squat for a while. Eldridge wasn't the booming little steel town it used to be, and up until now, Royce had been doing alright for himself in the meth trade. Unfortunately, the local Drug Task Force had shut down business, but he and Kristie had escaped right before the bust came.

They had been staying in the building for a few days. Royce only had a few hundred dollars and a bag of prescription pills to sell, something he did on the side. A cocktail of OxyContin and Adderall had inspired his sister Megan to come up with the idea to rob a house. Although they had broken into a residence, they had been too high to steal much more than candy and a Blu-Ray player.

Everything was where they had left it on the second floor. They had taken over a room by the hallway with access to both the stairs and the fire escape. After spending a day searching the building, other items had been found and carried up, including a small couch, two chairs, some old clothing used as pillows, flashlights, a pack of cards, and a few markers. Sleep had been rough the first night, but now they were burning through the Xanax supply. Royce had demanded that the girls stay off their cell phones, just in case they were being tracked, so instead they played a lot of card games. Megan was slowly filling the walls with marker doodles.

"Oh, I so need this chocolate right now," said Kristie, peering into the bag.

Megan snorted. "I know what you'll need in about two hours."

Kristie shot her a dirty look and went back to fiddling with the candy wrapper. The rail-thin blonde was a notorious bulimic, not to mention kind of a bitch. Megan didn't understand what her brother saw in her. She tried to play nice for Royce's sake, but sometimes it was just too easy not too.

"Why didn't we grab more stuff?" asked Royce in clear disgust.

"Timing?" offered Megan.

"This was all bullshit" roared Royce, hurling a candy bar across the room.

Neither of the girls said anything. Royce's temper had always been kept back by a hair-trigger, but it had randomly veered off into spontaneous rage the last few months. The slightest things set him off, for no apparent reason. It was best to just stay out of his way until he cooled down. Which in this case, was relatively quickly when he found a large bag of Skittles among his score.

"I wonder why they had so much candy," mused Megan.

"Kids?" said Kristie.

"Who cares?" said Royce, glancing over at Megan. "Can you go fill up the water jug again?"

Megan sighed. The water was still on in the building for some reason, but only in the basement bathroom. They had been filling up an old plastic gallon jug they had found and carrying it back to their room. This was fine, except it was now dark and the building could be officially creepy. Still, as Megan popped the second peanut butter cup in her mouth, she knew she was dying for a drink.

"Don't start crying," Kristie called out in a snarky voice.

"Don't start vomiting," she replied in the same.

Megan smiled as she heard Kristie swearing back in the room, but her smile quickly vanished as she descended the stairs. The flashlight didn't really help matters. In many ways, the minimal illumination only made things worse. It was like you knew that things were lurking right outside that small circle of light, things just waiting for you to shine your light elsewhere. So much could be in that surrounding blackness, such unknowns, behind you or to your sides. Megan rushed down the basement steps and turned the corner into the bathroom.

Checking the stall first, she turned and angled the gallon container as best she could under the sink's faucet. It filled halfway, the rest had to be filled with a few pours from an old coffee mug. Mission accomplished, Megan turned and made to race back up the stairs. She was taking a step up to ascend to the second floor when she stopped cold.

It was maybe twenty feet from the staircase to the large double doors that opened into what had once been some kind of lounge or gathering hall. A massive open space on the first floor that would accommodate a hundred people. There, in the scant moonlight coming in from the high arched windows, Megan saw someone walking across the floor. Without even having to think about it, she knew it wasn't Royce or Kristie. She watched silently for another moment as the figure strolled in the dark, then bolted upstairs as quietly as she could.

"Damn, that took you long enough," said Royce as soon as she burst into the room.

"And listen, I don't appreciate..." began Kristie.

"Shhh! Shut up," said Megan. "There's somebody downstairs!"

Kristie made a face. "No, there's not."

"Royce, I swear to you! There's some dude by himself, walking around in that lounge down there."

"Megan, don't fuck around."

Megan grabbed her brother by the face. "Someone. Is. Here."

Royce's eyes went wider. He stood up and walked to the couch. Reaching behind it, he pulled out a piece of slightly bent, three-foot long rebar.

"Stay here," he said.

* * *

Every step Royce took down the stairs made his anger grow. He had been driven out of his house, from his business and money, and forced to live like the shitstains he sold to. If he couldn't make those cops pay, he'd be fine with taking it out on someone else.

Royce looked around the first-floor landing and saw nothing, heard no one. He had left his flashlight upstairs, but there was enough moonlight coming in through the windows for him to see well enough. The whole place smelled moldy, like wet leaves. A few more steps and he was in the lounge, peering around.

It was maybe the size of a gymnasium, but squarer, lacquered wooden floors and four, high, cathedral-style windows on each side. At the far end, there looked to be a small stage built into the wall, complete with curtains. Now, the raised platform was just filled with scrap wood. Everything was silent, everything was still. There was no sign that anyone had been in here and Royce gripped the rebar tighter. He had never actually hit his sister, but this might be the first time.

"So it begins," came a voice from behind him.

Royce spun to see a man standing in the doorway. He was not what Royce had expected. Tall, with broad shoulders, he stood there completely concealed in a hooded cloak. Like one of those geeks playing dress up.

Royce lifted the rebar higher. "Who the fuck are you?"

"I am the Spittle, of the Ovessa."

Royce grimaced. "The what? What are you doing here? You with the cops?"

The man laughed. "Your authorities have no sway in these affairs."

"What?" asked Royce, shaking his head.

"It doesn't matter. Nothing matters but the swell of purpose, the gleam of vision. While you are but one of many, my beloved and I will see you all ground down."

"What the hell are you..."

Royce's words died off as the light began to flicker in his peripheral vision. It began to strobe, a cold white, and he felt the space behind him change. It grew warm, muggy, and fog began to swirl around his feet. The mechanical sounds of gears, chains, and pistons created a sort of industrial drum beat, one accented by moans and whispers.

Royce still hadn't turned, his eyes boring into the stranger.

"What?" was all he could ask once again.

"Turn and know," replied the Spittle.

Royce gripped the rebar and spun, ready to fight.

They were upon him before he had a chance to scream.

* * *

"He's been gone a really long time," said Megan.

"Yeah, but I'm not going after him when he's like this," said Kristie.

Megan folded her arms, displeased. Her brother had been gone almost twenty minutes and she hadn't heard anything. Not even him swearing at nothing in particular. That in itself worried her. Not so much for Royce, but more for her own wellbeing.

"I'm going after him," Megan declared as she got off the couch.

"Have fun with that."

"And when I find him, I'm gonna make sure to tell him that you didn't care enough to help me look," added Megan.

Kristie stared at her for a second. "You are such a bitch."

"Yes. Yes, I am. Now let's go."

There was not a sight nor sound of Royce as they crept down the staircase to the first floor. Both girls called out his name in whispering voices as they made their way up the hall to the front of the building. Here was an office, storage room, restroom, and an ornate antechamber. Nothing. No sign of him or anyone else.

Megan glanced over at Kristie and could tell the other girl was now getting freaked out. Megan wondered if he had gone down to the basement. Maybe he needed to hit the functioning restroom. She was going to be pissed if he was playing a trick on them. Plus, she *knew* she had seen someone in the lounge. The lounge, the last place to check on this floor.

As they snuck up to the opens doors that led to the open space, Megan saw someone standing in the center of the gloom. Without having to blink, she knew it wasn't her brother. Kristie, however, didn't seem to process what she was seeing as quickly and rushed toward him.

"Royce, you asshole, you had us scared to death! Where have you been?"

Kristie stopped two feet from the stranger, her arms out for an embrace, when he turned. He was big, well over six feet and broad in the shoulders. The hooded black cloak hid all of his features in the gloom, but Megan could swear she saw two pinpricks of red, glowing were his eyes should be.

"Not Royce," he said in a playful tone.

"Who..." tried Kristie as she stumbled back.

"I am the Spittle. I've been waiting for you both," he said, motioning for Megan to enter.

Megan cautiously came up behind Kristie. "Where's my brother?"

"Ah, he is currently under the gentle ministrations of the Invocated.

"The who?" squawked Kristie.

"Fear not. I assure you, you'll meet them soon enough yourself."

"Where's my brother?" Megan repeated.

"A brother, a lover. Such petty distinctions. I wonder which of you will be more determined?" he mused.

Megan opened her mouth for a retort when she realized that the light in the room was changing. The moonlight streaming through the windows was growing brighter while somehow the center of the room grew darker. The man in the cloak, calling himself "The Spittle," was awash in shadows, as was most of the floor. She reached out for Kristie when there was a flash, a burst of dull light that only lasted a second. Only a second, but it was long enough for Megan to see that the lounge was no longer empty. She froze, her fingers inches away from Kristie. What she had seen in that glimpse had defied reason.

Kristie, however, had seemingly witnessed nothing. She began screaming at the man, screeching to see Royce. Megan started to back away as his calm demeanor turned predatory.

"So it is the lover," he said with an edge to his voice. "You would be 'Kristie' then, correct?"

"How did you know my name?"

"Why, from Royce, of course."

He took a step back and threw his arms out wide, head titled back.

"All in the name of the Ovessa!" roared the Spittle, as if announcing it to the room.

The phantom illumination began to flash again.   It emanated from no particular source, simply bursting to life from various corners and at different intervals. A grey light, colder than white, it strobed and flickered, causing the scene to shudder. Some type of fog or smoke had slithered throughout the lounge, creating a haze. It brought with it a damp warmth that also carried a putrid stench. Sweat, sex, motor oil, and some type of chemical. It was overpowering.

The flashes brought to life a new panorama. Here, instead of an empty lounge, the space was filled with bizarre constructs made of metal. Surreal frames or exoskeletons, they were fashioned from all manner of materials. Many were roughly rectangular in shape and stood over twelve feet high, between them a variety of smaller esoteric devices or items. Everywhere lay blood-drenched canvases, some hanging off the tall constructions themselves.

Megan hadn't realized that music had started. It had just crept into her head and now she realized it was there. A cacophony so arrhythmic it was almost soothing. The sound of machinery and industry. Through it came the voices, the whispers and sighs. The moans.

The Spittle drifted back into the fog and others began to glide in and out of the metal monstrosities. All dressed in an assortment of rags, the tattered clothing was white and barely clung to their slender frames. Some were male, some female, many indeterminable. Their skin was coated with a slick sheen that looked thicker than sweat, more viscous. All of them bald, their faces were marred by horrific mutilation – lips, noses, ears, and eyelids all sliced off. Little more than flesh-covered skulls whispered their pledges and promises, threats and demands.

Rooted to the spot, Megan watched as they surrounded Kristie, cooing over her as they played with her hair and ran their fingers over her body. There was something wrong with their hands, too. Their fingers were too long, too pointed. It looked like their finger bones extended out past the nubs of flesh. The murmuring pack of mutilated creatures forced Kristie forward toward one of the taller metal frames that had a bloody sheet hanging from it. Kristie began to whimper as she neared it.

"You wish to be with him?" asked the Spittle, placing a hand on the blood-soaked linen. "Let us accommodate you."

He pulled it off, and there, hanging in the confines of the metal exoskeleton, Megan saw the sobbing thing that had once been her brother. She screamed because it was him and screamed because such an atrocity shouldn't be alive. Kristie screamed, too. But while they dragged Kristie closer to Royce, Megan stumbled backward, fell, and then ran.

She bolted out of the lounge and back to the stairs. Onto the landing, she hit the emergency exit and escaped out into the night. Megan kept running, block after block, until she couldn't breathe anymore. She had no idea what time it was, but everything looked closed downtown. Collapsing in an alleyway behind a pizza shop, she let the scent of sauce and pepperoni wash over her as she wept.

The idea that she had just escaped a gang of psychotic ghosts only made her head throb harder. That they had taken Royce was even worse. What was she supposed to do now?

Fortunately, she had grabbed her purse before coming downstairs. She had her cell phone and the keys to her apartment. She wasn't on the run like Royce and Kristie, she had only joined them for the excitement. This wasn't how she expected it to end. Her pragmatic side started pushing aside the horrors she had just witnessed. She could easily get a ride home or even walk from here. Probably call and get her job back at the mini-mart tomorrow. Her mom would assume Royce was on the run. How could she say otherwise? If forced to admit it, she wasn't too broken up about Kristie. She sat there contemplating it all for over an hour.

Exiting the alleyway, she started heading up the street and working on some believable lies. The closer to the truth, the better. She could easily say she woke up to find Royce and Kristie gone. Hell, even say they were crashing in that old building. She idly wondered if the ghosts would take their stuff.

So busy concocting a cover story, Megan didn't notice the fog that had begun to swirl around her. It grew thicker with each step, and the nearby appliance repair shop sign began to flicker. She froze, trying to convince herself that it was just a coincidence, as the stench wafted up to her.

The voice of the Spittle came through the darkness to her. "You cannot run. You belong to the Ovessa now."

Megan spun around, looking for him in the dense gloom. "No! I got out of the building, I escaped!"

"No, you didn't. You fled in your mind, but not in space," spoke his voice, dripping with amusement. "

"What are you? What do you want?"

Darkness became more tangible, shadows thickened. Flashes of light cut through, delineating new areas, creating new space. The fog rewove reality, building the metal structures and billowing out the bloody canvases. That unmistakable smell that had imprinted itself onto Megan's psyche drew her memory back, a memory of a place that was already here again. Its song of metal and whispers and moans began to play once more.

The Spittle strolled up to her, red eyes burning through the gloom of the hooded cloak. "We are everywhere, for we are outside. Outside your laws and your understanding, outside your science and your faith."

Leaning in, he was all smoldering ember eyes and gleaming teeth. The hood now drawn back, his hair flowed over his shoulders in black waves of ink. His body was composed of pieces of a white material, akin to bone or tooth. The body was held together by tendons and ligaments stretched across his frame. No muscles pulled, no skin covered him. He wasn't a ghost, he wasn't human.

He gestured and a structure behind him was revealed in full. Megan couldn't even take in a breath to vomit. Royce and Kristie hung side by side, living abominations somehow not allowed to die.

"Please," coughed out Royce from where he hung, suspended on a meat hook.

"No," replied the Spittle.

Megan felt her knees giving out. "Why?"

"You should be honored," said the Spittle. "My beloved believes you should be granted an audience with the divine."

"What? Which one..."

Then Megan saw her gliding through the fog. Another person in a black cloak, this time fully opened to reveal what lay beneath. A woman made of the same bone carapace, her hair cascading black liquid. She was beautiful, like a living statue, one awoken from the depths of hell.

Megan desperately attempted words, but nothing came.

"Humans are so fragile, so feeble, but will do anything to believe otherwise," said the woman as she stroked Megan's face. "Would you like something to believe in? Let us show you a truth."

Megan watched as the woman gestured up to where the ceiling used to be. The space spilt open and spilled out light, its glow felt as a weight upon her. It fell on Megan, consuming her. Repurposing her. The Invocated all around fell to their knees.

"For you are the Spittle," said the woman, as Megan was broken down.

"For you are the Sigh," the man replied to his beloved.

"All for the honor of the Ovessa."

CHAPTER 3

Texas had been relatively uneventful so far. Another stretch of shitty diners and worse motel rooms. Audrey wasn't necessarily having a bad time, but she wished she could be having more fun for Elliot's sake. They had stopped off at a little roadside attraction yesterday, filled with ceramic art and other handmade pieces from the area. Some of the pieces were actually quite nice, but not for the prices they were asking. All it had done was depress her, thinking about how she couldn't even afford a small trinket.

Today was a little better. They were cruising down the road, the sun was bright, and they were blaring The Smiths at high volume. She crooned along with the vocals between drags from her cigarette and tried not to think about her future. She'd quit smoking two years ago, but had picked it back up recently, fortunately keeping the quantity down. For some reason, they tasted better when she only had two a day, anyhow.

"We're gonna need gas soon," said Elliot over the music.

Audrey nodded and went back into her head. It still threw her that Elliot wanted anything to do with her. It turned out that their dad had always known about her, but he hadn't known that her mom had died. Audrey had been the product of a very short relationship between Melissa Darrow and Allan Byrnes, and when he had discovered that Melissa was pregnant, she told Allan she wanted nothing to do with him as a lover or husband or father to her baby. Dejected, he had moved on and met Elliot's mom. While Elliot's mother knew that Allan had another child out there, Elliot himself hadn't known until his father was dying. Allan Byrnes had developed cancer from working at a toxic waste incinerator, of all jobs. The lawsuit and subsequent settlement were funding the trip, something Elliot felt he should do with his sister. All Allan Byrnes knew after twenty-odd years was Audrey's name, but Elliot had tracked her down. To say their meeting had been awkward was an understatement.

Elliot obtained her email address through her website and persuaded her to meet. Not believing his story of being a long-lost brother, she arranged their meeting at her corner bar so she could have some liquid courage just in case. The husky, dark haired young man gave her pause, but those hazel eyes were the same she saw in the mirror every day. Elliot had been crushed to learn that her mother had died so long ago, that she had lived in foster care, and that he'd been denied his sister for all those years. He was so earnest, so kind, she couldn't help but feel a certain yearning to know him better. She cast aside her usual paranoia and proceeded to meet with Elliot about once a month as he finished his last year of college.

Then, two months ago, he proposed the road trip. A final gift from their father, something they could do together. Audrey had been hesitant to say the least, but he'd been so excited by the prospect. It took some juggling of finances to ensure her apartment would be there when she got back, but she had acquiesced.

"Oh, this place looks ridiculous. Let's stop here!"

Audrey glanced over and smiled. A gas station that looked like something out of a Hunter S. Thompson novel appeared on their left. The pumps hadn't been updated since sometime in the 1970's, and the storefront had a variety of bizarre tchotchkes hanging off its wooden porch roof. Immediately Audrey's imagination went to the family of cannibals that ran the joint and how they preyed upon unsuspecting travelers. The half a dozen or so cars parked out front didn't dissuade her from her fantasy.

Elliot parked the car and they both climbed out. He checked to make sure the pumps were actually operational and then went inside. Audrey paused to examine the items hanging from the roof. Dreamcatchers, wind chimes, decorative pieces, all kinds of things. A strikingly beautiful girl, pale and redheaded, about maybe fourteen, sat in a rocking chair carving a piece of wood on the porch. Audrey said hello, but the girl didn't seem to notice her.

The inside was exactly as she had pictured it. Average convenient store items like soda and chips stocked right next to animal pelts, tobacco pouches, and bowie knives. Audrey picked out an iced tea from a cooler and went to find Elliot at the counter. Waiting with him, she noticed a series of little carved wooden animals sitting on top of a glass case. They were simplistic, but all well-proportioned. Each one had been sanded, stained, and sealed.

The customer before them in line finished his transaction and Elliot stepped up. The man behind the counter looked tired but was quite friendly, thanking them for stopping in. Elliot paid for the gas and the beverages, and was about to walk away, when he noticed Audrey wasn't moving.

"These carving are beautiful. Are they done by the girl outside?"

"Yes, they're all done by my daughter," he said, beaming with pride.

"I'll take the owl," said Audrey, pulling her wallet out of her purse.

"Audrey, I can get that," said Elliot.

"You pay for enough, I've got this."

Audrey handed over a ten-dollar bill, the price for the small carved owl, and smiled as she cradled it in her hands. It made her happy knowing that girl had crafted it, probably right there on the porch, while her dad worked inside.

Elliot went to pump the gas, but she stopped by the girl again. Audrey watched her carve for a moment. The piece was still in the early stages and she couldn't yet make out what it was going to be. The girl was engrossed in her work, seemingly unaware of Audrey's presence.

"You do wonderful work," said Audrey. "I'm glad I bought this."

The girl paused and stared up at her. A look of confusion danced on her face for a moment until she spied the owl in Audrey's hands. Then it was a look more akin to sadness.

"I wish I was an owl. Do you wish you were an owl?"

"Um," tried Audrey.

"It would be meaningless then, all that darkness. Because it would belong to you."

"I guess so."

"But it's a little wooden toy. And we're just toys, dancing, screaming, and fucking. Pointless, except for the amusement of others."

Audrey gawked at the girl, trying to comprehend where these words were coming from, these nihilistic proclamations. The girl gave nothing away in her demeanor, utterly calm as these things fell from her mouth.

"This is going to be a badger. Badgers go into the dirt, and we all go into the dirt eventually. It's the way of things."

"Audrey?"

Audrey's head pulled away from the girl to see Elliot waving at her by the car. She turned back to see the girl go back to work on her carving.

"Um, thank you for making the carving."

"You're welcome," said the girl, not looking up. "Thank you for buying it."

Audrey walked off the porch, now feeling a distinct sense of dread for the small owl still cradled in her hands.

CHAPTER 4

Temperance Methodist Church had stood in Newton for over one hundred years. It was a small church and had never had a large congregation, but along with being the oldest church in the county, it also had its own cemetery. Equally small, with only around three hundred graves, the most recent dating back a good twenty years, it had run out of room long ago. While the church itself sat on top of a modest hill, the graves lined the hillside, some at a slope that would have been considered too precarious by other cemetery standards. They worked with what they had. The road and parking lot took up one side, residences on the left and right, and a small area of woods to the back. While the church had long sought to acquire a portion of the woods to make more room for the cemetery, the owner of the property had no desire to sell. Deer were plentiful, even in those few acres, come hunting season.

Only a few yards past the graves and into the woods, sat a pond. It was barely the size of backyard swimming pool, probably only twenty feet across in normal weather. Perpetually stagnant, nothing lived in its waters, no wildlife ever drank from its edge. It gave off a foul odor, as if something rotted deep within it. All of the plant life surrounding the pond had taken on a gelatinous appearance, as if everything was covered in a thin film of mold.

The few people who knew of the pond stayed away from it, fully aware that something was wrong with it. Rumors ranged from it being cursed to it being filled with toxic sludge. In a way, both were true. The pond was a place where reality was a bit looser, where physics began to breakdown.

There were many places like this around world, but it was from this pond that the man in the suit chose to rise.

He rose head first, straight up, water beading right off of him. Completely dry, he was dressed in a black suit with a grey shirt and black tie. He wore a red rose on his lapel. There was a bit of stubble on his face, less than on his head where his hair was cropped quite short. Dark hair, there was noticeable grey at his chin and temples. He was of average build, but he surveyed the woods with dark eyes that made him seem far more imposing.

Stepping across the pond, his feet splashed across the surface of the water then through the plants. None of the muck clung to him, none of the water soaked through. Continuing through the woods, he came out at the bottom of the hill and looked around at the cemetery. He frowned and began his way up the hill.

Billy Vicks, and his brother Bobby, had been tending the grounds at Temperance Methodist Church for years. They probably would have seen to burials too, had there still been room to bury anyone. Billy had been married in the church, Bobby still looking to settle down. They knew every parishioner in the church, so they were more than a little shocked to a see an unknown man, fully decked out in his Sunday best, walking through the cemetery on a late Thursday afternoon.

Bobby shut off his lawnmower and shouted out to the stranger. "Can I help you?"

The man either hadn't heard him or was ignoring him. Billy frowned and leaned his rake against the garbage can. He hoped this wasn't one of those weirdos who liked to hang out in cemeteries. Billy couldn't abide that kind of disrespect.

"You there, what's your business here?" Billy called out.

"My business? Well that's a complicated story, I'm afraid."

The man finished climbing the hill and came to stand a few paces away from Billy. Bobby jogged over to his brother, confused by the stranger's appearance. There was no car in the parking lot and he wasn't one of the neighbors. Nobody would walk that far in a suit like that in the summer.

"You can't just be wandering around here as you please," said Billy. "This is a reverent place."

"Isn't that exactly what you do in a reverent place," the man said with a smile. "You wander, seeking enlightenment. Silence and solitude among your dead. Is it not life-affirming?"

"What?" asked Bobby, confused.

"I don't know what you're babbling about, but if you're not a member of the congregation, I'm going to have to ask you to leave."

"Ah, flavors of faith. How remarkably petty and exclusionary. You do realize the dead no longer care about such things?"

"Listen here, fella..." began Billy, stepping forward.

"Listen? No, let me *show* you."

The world dropped out, reality breaking away. It was replaced with a never-ending blackness, a void so complete that it ate away at Billy just for daring to exist. A cold so sharp it drove knives into his psyche. The emptiness imploded, entropy made manifest, and in the corners of nothingness Billy saw the futility of reason, emotion, and humanity.

On earth, Bobby clutched onto his brother Billy as he lay on the ground, shaking and drooling.

"What did you do to him?" screamed Bobby.

"I simply opened his mind," replied the man in the suit.

Bobby tried to calm his brother, who was now pissing himself, his eyes rolling up into the back of his head. He had no idea what to do. He was going to have to run back to his truck to call for an ambulance. Laying Billy down as gently as he could, he sprinted to get his cell phone.

Running back, still on the phone, he realized the man was staring off into the distance, frowning. As if his brother didn't matter. Bobby felt the urge to punch the guy out, but he didn't want to end up like Billy. Instead he collapsed back down beside his brother, checking on him. He was still seizing.

Looking up, all Bobby could ask was, "Why?"

"Why?" said the man in the suit. "Because I wanted to."

The air around the man shimmered, like a heat distortion, but more angular. It shifted, and the man vanished. Gone.

Bobby stared down at what was left of his brother and started crying.

CHAPTER 5

The french fries were perfect. Crispy golden brown on the outside, seasoned just right, and fluffy potato goodness inside. Audrey had to consider that they may have been the best fries she'd ever had. Swiping another through the homemade cheese sauce, she popped it in her mouth. Elliot had gotten the same, but he was too busy attacking his giant burger.

"This may be the best food we've had on the trip so far," he said between mouthfuls.

She had to agree. Her grilled tofu dog had been served with peppers and onions, a delicacy even back in California. She had put sriracha sauce all over it, much to Elliot's horror. She thought back to the antacid medication he took every night and allowed herself a small smile.

A slight breeze blew, threatening their napkins. It was a beautiful day and they had decided to sit out on the patio and soak in the sun. At mid-afternoon, they had the space all to themselves. If this weather kept up, she might have to persuade Elliot to find a motel with a pool that night.

"So when did you decide to become a vegetarian?" asked Elliot, pointing at her tofu dog.

"I never really liked meat," she said. "Never liked the idea of it. But I didn't have much choice about what I ate when I was bouncing around foster care. Not until I went to live with the Reynolds. That was the summer before my freshman year in high school. They let me be vegetarian."

"So they were your parents through high school?"

Audrey slid another fry through her cheese sauce. "Parents? I guess you could call them that. They tried, best they could. I lived there with two other kids, I know I've told you about them. Duncan was a year older than me, Mandy was two years younger. Mandy was their precious baby and Duncan fought with them constantly. I was a ghost."

"I'm sorry," said Elliot.

Audrey didn't really want to go down that particular memory lane with her brother. It was more than just that the Reynolds ignored her, they didn't understand her. They understood Duncan and his anger, his need to lash out. He didn't trust anybody and made sure everyone knew it. Mandy, on the other hand, was a pampered little shit who sucked up to their foster parents at every available opportunity. She put on the shiny smile and was rewarded for it. Audrey just wanted to hide in her bedroom with her computer, conflict free.

Duncan had disappeared after he turned eighteen, not even bothering to graduate. Audrey had never seen him again. Mandy had fed off the Reynolds until the last possible moment before jumping ship. Last she heard, the young woman was much further south, down near Los Angeles. Audrey had graduated, got a job as a night stocker at an office supply warehouse, and moved into a studio apartment. She had gone back to visit the Reynolds once, but it had been an uncomfortable and tense hour. Never again.

"There had to be some good times with the Reynolds," said Elliot.

Audrey shrugged. "I suppose. They took us on a few short day trips. The beach, amusement parks, the zoo. The one trip to see their friend at the university was weird."

"University?"

"Yeah, I don't remember which one. We met some woman there. The Reynolds seemed friendly enough with her, but formal, too. Maybe like they were a little scared of her? I don't know. Professor Binici. She bought me a poster of the solar system."

"That's pretty cool."

"The whole thing was weird. They were weird. It's like they were desperate for us to be the picture book family. Day trips, family dinners, holiday photos, all of it. It was all so forced and fake."

'I don't know, like you said, they tried. You lost your mom to a violent car wreck, the other two had just been abandoned."

Audrey stared at him, wanted to scream, but knew he was right. Despite her foster parents bungling things, she always knew their hearts were in the right place. Even knowing that, she didn't want to hear it.

Elliot pushed the remains of his burger aside. "You never talk about her, you know."

"Who?"

"Your mom."

"What's to say? My mom was crazy and died in a wreck when I was seven."

"Audrey..." tried Elliot.

"It turns out she kept a dad from me. She used to lock herself in her room all the time and she would babble all kinds of insanity to me. I remember that. I remember being scared of her half the time."

"What would she say?"

Honestly, Audrey couldn't fully recall. She knew the things her mom had said all had a vaguely religious connotation to them, something fanatical. She didn't remember them ever going to church or to any type of service, but maybe Audrey was never present for these events. She just knew the words hadn't made much sense to her young mind and she had not found any answers since. All of her mother's possessions had been sold off to pay for her debts, those avenues of inquiry long gone.

Melissa Darrow had been insane. That's what Audrey had told herself for years, what she had likely believed even as a child when her mother was alive. She had denied Audrey her father, and then died suddenly, casting her young daughter into foster care. Whether the last was ultimately for better or worse, given her Mother's mental state, Audrey would never know.

"Audrey?"

She looked up at her brother, realizing she had drifted again. "Sorry, I don't want to talk about this anymore. Please?"

"Of course, I'm sorry."

She dipped two more fries in her cooling cheese sauce. Her brother. She was going to have to learn to be more open, for him if anything. She was too used to being alone. She had very few friends of note, and her last relationship had been a year ago and it had only lasted a few months. She needed to be better for Elliot.

"So where are we headed next?" asked Audrey.

CHAPTER 6

Eldridge, Ohio had once been grand, and the city elders mourned the decline of their town as often as they deluded themselves that it would rise again. A part of the so-called "rust belt," it had lost a great deal of industry jobs overseas in the 1980's and never found anything to replace them. Two massive steel plants at the edge of town sat empty, constant reminders of what used to be.

Decades ago, the city had thrived. The streets and buildings had been well-tended, the schools over-flowing, and the businesses prosperous. Not any longer. Pot holes lined every roadway, no money available in the meager budget to fix them, and most of the expensive stoplights had been replaced with stop signs over time. Not that it mattered, the traffic had dwindled along with the population. There were as many vacant homes as there were vacant storefronts, many of them filthy and falling apart. The city would tear down condemned buildings where it could, but the offending structures numbered in the hundreds. Eldridge City Schools enrollment had dropped alarmingly over the years, parents shipping their children to neighboring districts or moving out of the county altogether. People had no money to spend, so more and more businesses closed every year. A majority of the downtown was boarded up, the restaurants, boutiques, salons, book stores, haberdasheries, coffee shops, and more all having closed their doors for good.

The Wiltshire Hotel had been one of the jewels of Eldridge, a four-story building with a finished basement and complete with kitchen, dining hall, lounge, and ballroom. While it only had thirty small rooms in the building, it had been considered the premiere accommodation in the city during its time, from its completion in the 1930's through the 1960's. Poor management had seen it fumble in the seventies, and by the time The Wiltshire was on its feet again a decade later, there was no one left to rent out a room.

Various entrepreneurs had attempted to purchase the building in hopes of revitalizing the property over the years, but nothing ever came of it. It was too old, too big, too run down. Its size was a factor for the city, too cost prohibitive to bother tearing down. So instead, it sat there empty, another dead dream of the past.

Or it had been empty, until recently.

* * *

Heather wasn't sure what was happening. She could barely remember how she got into the building. Driving home from work at the office, she was cutting through town when she had pulled over for some reason. No reason. Right in front of the old hotel. Something had compelled her to get out of her car and wander to the side of the building. There was a utility door there, one she had found unlocked. Heather didn't know why she had to go inside, but she did. Dust motes floated in the dying sunlight which provided just enough light for her to see the stairs. She took them, still wondering what she was doing.

The place was relatively untouched, except for the years of accumulated grime. There wasn't any litter or graffiti. Hand-carved banisters made from fumed oak wrapped around the stairs, small chandeliers at every landing. Heather kept rising, her destination unknown. On the third floor she froze, listening. Sounds leaked out from one of the rooms, something that sounded like sobbing.

Was someone here? What was *she* doing here? For a moment, Heather was petrified with indecision. Everything inside her told her to run, to flee from the darkening hotel. Instead, she took another step up and continued to the fourth floor. Screaming in her mind, she left the sounds behind her.

At the final landing, the hallway turned left toward a room or right into some sort of antechamber. Compelled, she moved right, and the stench hit her. Putrid, it smelled like body odor with some kind of chemical on top. Against her will, she pushed open both of the double doors and stepped into madness.

It had been a ballroom once, long ago. Square, with high ceilings, and a stage for a band at the back. Now, it was filled with a dull, pulsing light that illuminated skeletal-like mechanical structures that held aloft dozens of people clad in white. They laughed and wept, babbled and prayed. All of them were disfigured beyond recognition, all identically so. Scurrying about the metal lattice work as if it were a jungle gym, they watched as Heather walked beneath them, dripping blood and saliva on her. Even now, she still couldn't scream.

On the stage stood two figures clad in black robes. Heather found herself on her knees before them. Tears burst from her eyes, the only expression of terror she could release.

"Another one, my beloved," said the shorter of the two, her voice feminine.

"Another to be repurposed," added the other cloaked individual.

"Perhaps," said the woman, drawing back her hood. "Perhaps we should test the mettle of our first Invocated in this realm."

Heather choked at the site of the woman. She looked like a demonic statute come to life. Her skin was more like an ivory shell, shifting plates over internal organs held together by visible connective tissue. The blackest water splashed down from her head and off her shoulders in place of hair, her red eyes burned in amusement.

"The Sigh of the Ovessa speaks wisely, as always," said the man.

He gestured and one of the mutilated people crept forward. It had been a young woman once. Once, before most of its hair had been ripped out, its lips carved off, its nose cut off, its eyelids and ears shorn from its body. Once, before its fingers had been extended and the flesh whittled away so that the bones protruded from the ends in sharpened points. Once, before it was smeared with some type of viscous substance that clung to its body, some of its muscles greying and fungal, and then clad in white rags. Once, it had been the junkie's sister Megan.

"You are going to run," said the woman. "If you can make it outside, you are free. But you have only moments before this Invocated gives chase. I would be swift."

Heather looked from the woman to the creature standing near her.

"Go!"

Without looking back, Heather spun and sprinted for the exit. She banged the double doors open and fumbled her way down the stairs. The spell now broken, sobs came quickly, and tears clouded her eyes. She twisted around the landing and lost a shoe. Kicking off the other one, she kept going. She rounded the second-floor landing when she heard a bang from above. Not even bothering to look, she took the next few steps as fast as she could.

The blow hit her from behind so hard she lost her breath. She fell, rolling to the first-floor landing. Only feet away from the door, she tried to get up when a pain shot through her leg. Heather screamed out and reached back to find wetness. Blood. She rolled over to see the creature on its haunches only feet away.

"Please," began Heather.

The thing that had been Megan dove and buried its mouth in Heather's throat, tearing it apart. Between its claws digging away, and its teeth, it gored Heather's neck down to the spine, ripping it asunder with a strong yank. Holding the severed head it its hands, it peered up to where the Spittle and the Sigh stood on the landing.

"Yes," said the Sigh. "That will do."

CHAPTER 7

The bar was much like any other and Audrey was grateful for that. She didn't go for those themed places or anything too upscale. All she needed was a place to serve her drinks at a decent price and not harass her. This resort was one of the only nicer stops that Elliot had planned, and she had been worried about the atmosphere of the place. Turned out it was just a low-key spa and casino, with a restaurant and bar. All that really mattered to her was the bar.

She didn't want Elliot to know how much she drank. It wasn't an everyday thing, but it was definitely an every *other* day thing. She knew it was connected to her depression. When you spend a weekend consuming nothing but Oreos and wine while streaming Buffy reruns, you know you have a problem. She was self-medicating, only because real medication was too expensive.

She'd only drank twice so far on the trip and she was proud of that. To celebrate, she planned on getting tanked tonight. The real world was weighing on her this evening, responsibilities waiting for her back home and lack thereof.

Taking a sip of her beer, Audrey wondered what she'd be doing if she were back in California right now. Probably sitting at home, drinking a beer, and sitting on the computer. She spent a lot of time in various geek forums, arguing pointless movie trivia. The internet was a nice buffer for her, although sometimes it made her feel lonelier than it did connected.

An internet forum was how she met her last boyfriend, Kyle. They had the same interests in computers, science fiction, and vegetarianism. At first it had seemed great, someone so similar, but Audrey quickly learned that he was looking for something far more serious than she was, plans that involved marriage and kids down the road. She was only looking to hang out, maybe get laid. The whole relationship had quickly dissolved, especially when Kyle accused her of being an alcoholic.

Yes, she most likely drank too much. And yes, she probably should have opened up to him more about her past. But it wasn't Kyle's job to "fix" her, to mold her into something he wanted. The whole thing had both made her sad and pissed her off in equal measure.

Speaking of guys, Audrey noticed the guy at the end of the bar smiling at her again. An older guy in a suit. Was that a rose in lapel? Weird. Still, he was quite handsome for a guy in his forties.

Intellectually, Audrey knew she was attractive, even if she rarely felt it. A petite five-foot-one with curvy measurements, wavy blonde hair cut right below her shoulders, olive complexion, and green eyes. She wasn't wearing anything special tonight, but the cutoff jean shorts and white tank top did show off a lot of skin. The blistering heat had dictated her outfit more than any desire to be sexy.

Today was the first day Elliot had worn something other than a T-shirt, now sporting a black polo. Of course, he wore it with camouflage cargo shorts and flip-flops.

"We should do shots," said Elliot.

"If you insist," replied Audrey.

He ordered two shots of tequila with salt and lemon.

She frowned at the drinking accessories and picked up the shot. "We don't need training wheels."

Elliot laughed and downed the shot with his sister.

She took a swig from her beer. "Is there anything you wanted to do here? Gamble or get a seaweed facial?"

"Nope, it was just along the way and I thought we could crash here for the night. It really wasn't all that much more expensive."

"That's surprising."

He shrugged and changed the subject. "That guy over there seems to be checking you out."

Audrey glanced over to see the older gentleman at the end of the bar smiling at her. He had a certain Hollywood look to him, like one of those stylish actors poured into a suit come Oscar season. He raised his glass and nodded at her. Unsure what to do, she smiled back and tipped her own bottle toward him.

"Wow, you're not very good at that, are you?"

"Shut up, Elliot."

"Go talk to him."

"We're in some random town in... wait, we're not even in Texas anymore, are we? I don't even know what state we're in. I'm not going to go flirt with a stranger I just met in a bar halfway across the country."

"Well, it doesn't matter now. He's gone."

Audrey spun back in her chair to stare at the spot where the man in the suit had been. Sure enough, he'd left. For some reason, his departure made her sad. Although it had been nothing, his smile had brightened her night.

As that thought passed through her mind, she got more depressed. The smile of a stranger was the highlight of her day. That was her life. Twenty-four years old and so very little to show for it. She felt that familiar void opening up and called on the bartender to bring more beers and another round of shots.

"You okay?" asked Elliot.

How did she answer that? No, she was wreck, her life was pointless? She had to try to stay upbeat for Elliot, or at least put up that front. He deserved that from her. No matter what came up on this trip, she would endure.

"I'm fine, just ready to drink my baby brother under the table."

Elliot's face broke into a big grin. She never referred to him in such sentimental terms, finding them uncomfortable.

But she knew he wanted that from her, that he wanted that bond. Drinking was definitely a bonding exercise she could get behind.

"More shots then," he said. "Whiskey this time?"

"Bring it."

CHAPTER 8

The coffee machine dripped more of its precious black liquid into the pot, filling the kitchen with a rich aroma. It was already late, but Emily Binici needed the caffeine to stay awake. There were still too many unknown variables at play.

Pouring herself a cup, she added a splash of hazelnut creamer and allowed the aroma to drift up to her. Carrying it back to her office, she sipped and wondered to where her cat had disappeared. Likely sleeping somewhere. Another sip and Binici frowned at the pile of books on her desk. So far everything she had read was leading her to negative speculations.

Binici had been a professor of Cultural Anthropology for over thirty years. She had taught at two different California universities and was now tenured. Most of her published work surrounded cultural adaptations of The Sacred Feminine, although she had done studies on a variety of other topics including Blood Rituals, Chthonic Appropriation, and Fertility Ceremonies. Unknown to most in academia, this made her the foremost expert on something called the Crimsonata.

What even less of them knew, the Crimsonata was real.

She had stumbled upon it near the beginning of her career while cross-referencing numerous accounts from lesser-known cultures. They spoke of a woman who communed with the gods through her blood. This woman was sometimes an oracle, sometimes a witch, and sometimes thought divine herself. Always it was believed that her blood somehow appeased the gods of that particular culture, although the how and why was never clear. Binici had dove into these myths, pulling apart fact from fiction. She found more than she would have ever thought possible.

There was some truth to the lore, a lineage that traced back millennia. It had ties, in some ways, to all the major religions, a host of well-known legends. What was more disturbing, it opened up the possibility of so many more ideas that had been regarded as fantastic to be considered more carefully. The world was not exactly as we believed it was with our science and rational minds.

Along the way, Binici had made some strange friends. She had discovered that she wasn't the only person who had stumbled onto a secret truth. While these people could be intimidating, they could also be quite useful. It was through their aid that she had tracked the lineage of the Crimsonata. It had taken a considerable amount of time and the results weren't exactly satisfactory.

The last Crimsonata had died in a car crash and her heir had only been a child. Binici had met the child, Audrey Darrow, but she seemed an unremarkable girl. If Audrey knew anything of the potential within her, she didn't show it. Considering the young age of the Darrow girl at the time of her mother's death, it was likely that no great wisdom had been passed down. At the time, Binici had wrote it off as an opportunity missed.

But that was almost a decade ago, and now, things had changed.

Binici took another sip of her coffee and opened her laptop. Pulling up a spreadsheet, she examined the document and sighed. Time was not on their side. Reaching for her cellphone, she retrieved a slip of paper from inside her desk drawer.

The other end answered on the third ring. "Hello?"

"Dr. Faure? It's Emily Binici."

There was a pause. "It's late Emily. Is everything alright?"

Binici looked at the clock and swore to herself. She forgot about the time difference he would have there in Illinois.

Unfortunately, she needed the Comparative Religions professor, and this wouldn't wait until morning.

"Have you heard anything?" she asked.

"Yes, it's worse than we thought," he replied in a hushed voice. "There're reports of degradation all across the country. Probably the world."

"My research can only go so far, but it's what I feared. It's been too long since the Crimsonata flowed. Any longer threatens permanent damage, and possible seepage."

"That's... unacceptable."

Binici sighed. She hated what she was about to say, what she was sentencing that girl to, but the alternative was unthinkable.

"Contact the Promethean Wall," said Binici. "Tell them to use their contacts to find Audrey Lynn Darrow. The Crimsonata must be forced to flow."

"I'll leave tonight," said Faure before hanging up.

Binici stared at her phone, trying not to think about what she had just condemned Audrey Darrow to. She tried to justify it to herself, saying that being the Crimsonata was Audrey's birthright, which had her mother not died, she'd be flowing now. Binici was only ensuring the natural balance. For all she knew, it could be a wonderful experience being the Crimsonata, something the young woman would thank her for.

Binici didn't believe any of that.

They didn't have much time. The barriers between realms were breaking down. Soon there would be nothing holding back the hordes below or the glory from above. The earth would be shattered in the ensuing chaos, all the Outer Kingdoms attempting to cohabitate in one singular space simultaneously.

She hoped the Promethean Wall understood their duty in this situation. Killing the young woman would be disastrous, they had to use her to stop a greater plague. The Wall was efficient, but often over-zealous. She'd only met a handful in person, and if Binici was being honest with herself, they scared her.

Back in the kitchen, she poured the remainder of her coffee down the sink. She already knew she wasn't going to sleep tonight, she could feel it. She wondered what Audrey Darrow was doing and hoped the young woman's last few days of freedom were good ones.

CHAPTER 9

The night had cooled down and the stars were out in the clear sky. The bar had begun to thin out a bit, but the casino was still doing brisk business next door, the time of day no concern to those gambling away their money. Audrey lit up a cigarette, pleasantly hammered. She would have a hangover in the morning, but she wasn't so wasted that it would be painful. Even now she could walk straight if she put her mind to it.

Elliot staggered up next to her and made a child-like grabbing motion that she took to mean he wanted to bum a smoke. Raising an eyebrow, she pulled one out of the pack and handed it to him. It took him a full minute to get the thing lit, finally coughing out a lungful when he did. Not saying anything, she stood beside him and they both swayed back and forth slightly.

"For a tiny thing, you can hold your liquor," Elliot finally said.

"Willpower," she replied.

"Will you make fun of me if I throw up?"

"Nope. We drank a prestigious amount."

"Cool."

Audrey felt the giggles coming on, a sensation she rarely got when drunk. It occurred to her that this exact scenario would have played out countless times had they grown up together. As Elliot's older sister, she would've been the one to get him into upper class parties and sneak him beers. She would've been the one to take him out for his twenty-first birthday and get him smashed. They had missed out on all of those memories, but at least now they had this one.

Out in the parking lot, someone weaved among the cars, obviously drunk and probably forgetting where they had parked. Audrey hoped they weren't driving. She was glad their room was on the first floor. She wasn't sure if she could navigate stairs too well and an elevator might make her feel like Elliot looked.

"Where do we go tomorrow?" Audrey asked, trying to get his mind off his stomach.

"We keep heading east awhile. Soon we will have to decide if we want to shoot north or carry on to the coast. Doesn't matter to me."

"I wouldn't mind..."

"Doesn't matter to meee!"

"Wow, you really are drunk."

She laughed and glanced back out to the parking lot. The drunk patron had made their way closer to them. She winced as the person banged off an SUV's driver's side mirror. Looking around, there were other people going in and out of the casino, two more people standing on the other side of the bar entrance smoking, but nobody noticed the drunk. Audrey tried to shrug it off.

"I need to eat something," said Elliot.

"You think that's a good idea?"

"Yeah, something in me besides booze."

"Okay, I think that buffet in the casino is all night. I don't know."

"Hey Audrey?"

"Yes?"

"I think that chick is all fucked up."

Audrey's head turned from Elliot to where he was pointing. The person she had mistaken for a drunk came lurching out from between the cars. Not drunk, destroyed. Most of her white outfit was in tatters and much of the remainder showed a bruised body. Perhaps some kind of car accident, her face looked ruined, the lower portion of it gone and her eyes wide. Arms that look broken hung limply at her sides, something wrong with her hands.

The sight of the woman was alarming, terrible, but something about those hands jarred a portion of Audrey's psyche. It looked too deliberate, too perfectly achieved. The woman's eyes were still stretched wide. Within seconds of seeing her, Audrey's compassion evaporated under her paranoia.

"Jesus, are you okay?" asked Elliot, starting forward.

"Elliot, stay back," said Audrey, grabbing his shirt.

The other two people smoking outside had also seen the woman, but hadn't the same suspicions as did Audrey. They immediately rushed over to her. Both looked to be business men, about a decade older than her and Elliot. The first one got backhanded across the parking lot. What Audrey now realized were claws gored his face in the blow. The second backed up, but not fast enough. The woman leapt upon him and shoved her face into his throat. Sprays of blood arced through the air as she rode him down to the asphalt.

By this point, people coming and going from the casino had heard the commotion and walked over. The smart ones ran as soon as they saw the bloodshed. A security guard raced over and threatened the woman with a Taser, but he seemed terrified to use it. The woman drew closer to Audrey and Elliot.

"Get back!" said Elliot, putting himself between Audrey and the woman.

The monstrosity took a swipe at him and tore into his arm. He let out a cry and stumbled back, pushing Audrey into a potted tree. She fell over, the woman looming above her.

And then the creature exploded.

A shower of flesh and viscera rained down all over the place, coating everyone. Audrey was too shocked to care. She was sure that the woman was about to kill her, that she was about to die. She crawled over to Elliot who was on his knees, vomiting beside the tree. He wasn't the only one. The inept security guard was doing the same between two cars. A few other witnesses had been covered in gore, along with the two victims of the attack.

But the man in the suit with the rose in his lapel wasn't. He stood there, perfectly clean, staring at her. She returned his gaze, seeking answers, but only got a slight nod. Elliot groaned, and Audrey only looked away for a second, but when she looked back, the man was gone. Gone at an impossible speed.

She helped her brother up as the siren came roaring through the night, a headache beginning to form at the base of her skull. Too much, too fast. Audrey wasn't good at processing like this. She had no answers herself, let alone to give anyone else.

CHAPTER 10

It had been a long night of questions and speculations. The police had arrived with ambulance crews following close behind. Elliot had stood there, even after everything, still far too drunk to fully process what was happening. The trigger-happy sheriff's deputies had pulled guns on the witnesses and forced them all down onto the ground. Fortunately cooler heads within the EMTs prevailed.

Elliot found himself led away to the back of an ambulance where an older woman with a long brown ponytail tended to him. At first, she and her partner thought Elliot was more severely injured. Then they realized the gore covering him wasn't his own.

"What the hell happened here?" the medic asked as she cleaned out the wound on Elliot's arm.

"Some crazy woman, all fucked up looking. We were just standing outside smoking when she attacked all of us. And then, then she blew up!"

The EMT handed Elliot a packet of ibuprofen that he swallowed down with some bottled water. She explained that she didn't want to give him anything stronger until he sobered up. Her partner waved over one of the deputies who wore a deep frown. Elliot was asked to tell his story again to the deputy who listened, his eyes narrowing.

"That's pretty much the same account we're getting from everyone, even from the patrons who were far enough away not to get splattered. Unfortunately, all of our witnesses were drunk, so we're having a little trouble getting a reliable account of what this woman looked like."

"I'm telling you, she was missing half her face!" tried Elliot.

"Uh-huh. Or she had a Halloween mask on."

It continued on like that for most of the night. The sheriff himself finally arrived and wasn't much more understanding. As far as the authorities were concerned, some lunatic in a mask had shown up and attacked a bunch of people before blowing herself up with what they assumed had been a suicide vest. There was no evidence of a suicide vest, but that was the theory they were sticking to. The victims of the attack were treated as probable co-conspirators and kept separated, forbidden to clean themselves up until dawn arrived. They were only released when the owner of the resort showed up and had some stern words with the sheriff behind his car.

Elliot shuffled over to Audrey, his head throbbing. He had picked most of the larger bits off, but there was still a film of blood coating him. She stood beside the potted plant where he had been forced to leave her, chain smoking. The sheriff walked up to them, his face set in a scowl.

"You're free to go for now, but I don't want you going far," the sheriff said.

Elliot opened his mouth to agree when Audrey interrupted. "Bullshit. Either arrest us now or we are free to go. Period. We're from California and we're not saying here."

"The resort has agreed to put you up for free," growled the sheriff.

"I don't care," said Audrey. "My brother and I were just attacked, blown up on, and then treated like criminals for over six hours. If you don't want us to leave, arrest us."

The sheriff sneered and stormed away. Cursing under her breath, her hand shaking, Audrey took another puff of her cigarette. Elliot had never seen that side of her and didn't know what to say. However, he did know what she wanted.

"We can leave for California in a few hours, after some sleep."

"I don't care where we go, Elliot, I just refuse to stay here."

"The sheriff isn't..."

"Fuck the sheriff, I don't care about some god 'ol boy," she said. "I don't know what the hell happened here tonight, but it scared me. Badly. And I want as far away from here as possible."

He reached over and slipped the pack of cigarettes from her hand, pulling one out for himself. Lighting it, he tried not to examine her too obviously. While the events of the night had definitely frightened him, they seemed to have affected Audrey much more deeply. Her eyes kept darting around the parking lot as if seeking out another would be monster to come creeping. He didn't know how she could still be so tense after so many hours. Her right index finger tapped manically away at the cigarette pack after he handed it back.

"We'll go anywhere you want," he said. "Just let me get cleaned up and grab a few hours of sleep."

"Okay," she said, nodding a little too aggressively.

Since the first time he had met her, Elliot knew his sister had battled her own demons. Everyone did, but hers always seemed so much sadder, sharper. He knew he was a goofy, upbeat guy and part of him wanted to bring some of that light into Audrey's life. She deserved it, after the life she had lived. Long-lost younger sibling or not, he wanted to take care of her.

He wouldn't tell her of his suspicions, his fears. He wouldn't tell Audrey that when he thought back to those moments in the parking lot, when that woman was attacking them, that it seemed to be coming for her. She didn't need to hear that, especially when he kept telling himself that it was probably just his drunken imagination.

He didn't imagine the man in the suit, though. He had been standing there right before the woman had exploded, and Elliot would swear that he was there after, too. Except he wasn't covered in her remains, he was still clean and calm. He knew he saw the man from the bar, but it had all happened so fast.

It didn't matter. Audrey wanted to leave, and they would. They'd go east toward the coast and up toward New York. Whatever it took to keep her happy, make her feel safe.

CHAPTER 11

Robert Tyler often thought his job as principal at Eldridge High School would be much more preferable if there weren't any students to deal with. They were unruly, immature, and hormonal. Tyler demanded control in all aspects of his life and that definitely applied to his role at the school. He had openly laughed at the idea of "students' rights," appalled by the notion. As far as he was concerned, school was there not only to educate, but to break children of willful disobedience so that they could be productive members of the system. If you knew your place and played your role, the system always worked.

Tyler had believed in that whole-heartedly until he found himself chained naked to what looked like a piece of scaffolding in the old Wiltshire Hotel.

He didn't know how he had gotten there, but he knew what was happening now. Information was leaking into him, filling his head. He was learning, being prepared. Either of two fates awaited him after his repurposing – fodder or existence as one of the Invocated.

The air was thick and oily, filled with a haze. Below, he could still make out moving things, creatures that were far from human. Something that looked like an eyeball the size of beach ball slithered past on a mass of tentacles. It left a trail of slime in its wake. A tri-pedal beast with a gaping maw lumbered up and removed a whimpering man from the metal structure Tyler was shackled to, carrying him over to a table that looked to be made of meat. He was glad he couldn't see far enough to tell what was happening when the thing with dozens of spider legs lowered itself over the man. He could still hear the screams, though.

Bio-engineering, terraforming, invasion. Tyler knew these creatures had come from elsewhere, somewhere lower. They had always been aware of Earth, watching it, waiting. Something had finally changed, and they were taking the opportunity to strike. He knew it because he also knew that something throbbed floors above him, something barely yet materialized. It wanted Robert Tyler to know that he was nothing, just animated meat.

The Ovessa thrust and bucked against the barrier that still held it out. The serpentine star of illuminated flesh, it would rule over Earth as it did its own realm. A place where organic matter wasn't confined, wasn't distinct. It's why the Ovessa found Earth so fascinating, the idea of individual life. Everything was bound to it there, part of it. Most of the monstrosities that inhabited the Wiltshire had been formed for the first time when coming here.

At least, in their present forms. Two creatures masquerading in human form strolled into the room, clad in black cloaks. Tyler knew they were the Ovessa's emissaries. the Spittle and the Sigh. Their titles were simply approximations of what their divine being saw as the creative process. Having lurked at the edge of the world's consciousness for eons, biding their time and eager for the opportunity, they enjoyed both the chance at having names and the chance to do such holy work.

"The Invocated we sent after the Crimsonata was defeated," said the Sigh. "Obliterated."

"It would seem we underestimated her," said the Spittle.

"Perhaps. I was not aware that a human entity possessed such offensive capabilities."

"The Ovessa sees less as it prepares for the breaking of the barriers. We may not know what happened, but it's of little concern. Are we able to send any of our other kin yet?"

The Sigh's liquid black hair trickled over her shoulders. "No, not yet. However, I believe we will attack the Crimsonata in another fashion until we gain the strength for a more direct assault."

Tyler heard these words, but they meant nothing to him. Very little did now. Everything in which he had believed turned out to be empty. All of his notions of control had been illusions, just something he had told himself to sleep better at night. But the Ovessa *was* control, complete order. Free of chaotic humanity, he would be nothing more than an extension of will, an automaton of flesh. Tyler welcomed it. It didn't occur to him that his thoughts on the matter were the thoughts of the Ovessa.

The Tri-pedal creature lumbered over to him. It occurred to Tyler that the thing resembled some bastard offspring of a bear and a trout. Removing him from the shackles, it didn't even occur to him to struggle. Carried to the meat table, the spider-like attendant shuddered and two more of its kind appeared to the sides. One held a cluster of what appeared to be mushrooms.

He felt them remove sections of his body, entire chunks of muscle and whole sheets of skin. The pain was there, intense, and yet he took it gladly. It was all in honor of the Ovessa. The fungus was packed into these wounds and smoothed out, the rest of it mushed into a paste and painted over his body. He felt his genitals sliced off and the fungus sealing him into a eunuch. His hair was ripped out and his lips, nose, eyelids, and ears were carved off. A thin layer of the paste coated his whole head. Two balls of gelatinous material were placed onto the table and his fingers inserted. The tips began to swell and lengthen, their growth facilitated by the properties of the gel. After a few moments, his hands were withdrawn, and the balls were removed, the fingers each now three inches longer. Flesh was carved away down to the bone and those bone tips sharpened like the razor-like talons of the spider-things. Finally, the thing that had been Robert Tyler was adorned in white wrappings and rags, cloth spun and woven by the spider-things themselves.

Everything that had been Robert Tyler was gone. Personality, individuality, sanity – all of it had been shorn away in the process of becoming an Invocated. Now he was just another of many, many that now numbered in the hundreds in Eldridge.

All in the honor of the Ovessa.

CHAPTER 12

It was still raining. Timothy Faure had been driving all night and that the storm followed him he took to be an ill omen. He turned up the Tchaikovsky in his car, not only to stay awake, but to drive off his superstitions. It wasn't much farther now.

Faure, much like Binici, had been sucked into a hidden fringe world thanks to his academic research. He had been fascinated with what he called "micro-cults," small pockets of four to ten people that seemed to band together around any number of belief systems for short periods of time. Other scholars had done some study on the topic, but he believed there was something more to the phenomena, something that thematically linked most, if not all, of the groups together. He had talked to many members of various cults over his decades, received numerous answers, but it had been a young woman outside of Tampa who had set him on a different track.

Her name was Sally and she was another of the many disenfranchised youth that Faure often met with. Someone seeking answers that they hadn't found in traditional forms of organized religion. Sally's little cult was different from most, however, and she was its lone survivor.

Pale and thin, with stringy brown hair, she had been a nobody. Ignored, forgotten. She fiddled with a sugar packet as she told Faure how her cult, the Radiant Eye, had acquired a very peculiar talisman through dubious means in Shreveport. All the members of the cult had become addicted to the power it gave them, abilities like telepathy and telekinesis. They grew bolder as they grew in strength, lashing out at those they perceived had wronged them. The only reason she had survived the massacre was because she had to work late at the grocery store one night.

Faure had found her tale too fantastic for belief. Magical powers granted by some artifact? Where was this talisman now? Taken by the people who had murdered her friends, people who called themselves the Promethean Wall. They said they were protecting humanity from supernatural forces, from people like her. They only left her alive out of spite as far as Sally was concerned.

The Promethean Wall. A cursory glance showed nothing, a blank on the name. But something had stuck with Faure, a nagging sensation that more information might be found. He hadn't believed Sally's story about magic powers, but it was a recorded fact that her friends were found dead in the cabin. While it had been chalked up to ritualistic suicide, he wondered if perhaps murder might have been at play. Talented at tracking down information from the barest of leads, it didn't take long for the vast conspiracy of the Wall to come tumbling out into the light.

That had been almost a decade ago.

Faure eyed the large house as he pulled up into the driveway. He'd only been to this particular safe house once, years ago. It was a three-story red brick affair, with peeling white shutters, the whole place appearing ready to fall apart. Vines clung to the side of the house, creeping up the brick and across a porch roof that badly needed re-shingled. A window in the upper floor was broken out and had been hastily repaired with cardboard and tape, the window next to it was cracked. The driveway was filled with ruts and what little yard there was had been left mostly unattended and overgrown.

With a sigh, he climbed out and made his way to the front door. He didn't even have a chance to knock before the door was opened by a massive man in jeans and a T-shirt. Clean-shaven and square jawed, his thick black hair hung loose to frame a scowling face.

Faure touched the back of his closed fist to his forehead. "I'm here for the Wall."

The man snorted and walked away from the door, leaving it open. Realizing that it was as good an invitation as he was going to get, Faure followed the man inside. The furnishings were as Spartan as he remembered, nothing on the walls for decoration, only a few threadbare couches and a plain stand for a television. A dining room table held an impressive array of computer equipment, far more than would be needed for a normal gathering of people.

A thin, scruffy looking man in his late forties came in from the kitchen, drying off him hands on a towel, while a young woman with a long dark hair and a caramel complexion came down the stairs. Both of them peered at him warily.

"Who are you?" asked the big man, motioning Faure to sit.

"I'm Dr. Timothy Faure. I thought Dwight operated this cell."

"Dwight's dead."

"Jesus," mumbled Faure. "I didn't know. When?"

"About a year ago."

Faure rubbed his temples. "That, that doesn't change anything. I run level two intel for the Wall and I have a priority assignment."

The big man smirked. "Do you now?"

"What's your name, sir?"

"I'm Hayden. That's Greer and Roma," he said, nodding toward the thin man and the woman respectively.

"Mr. Hayden, I'm sure you're aware of the uptick in activity these last few weeks. It has skyrocketed in the last few days. I know exactly why and how to stop it."

Hayden didn't look impressed, but the woman named Roma leaned forward. "What can you tell us?"

"As far as we can tell, for at least seven thousand years, there has been a lineage of women who possess a unique metaphysical ability. Called the Crimsonata, sometimes there were more than one of these women in existence, many in fact, but sometimes only one. Despite their numbers, the Crimsonata always did as she was supposed to do – she flowed. Her very purpose is to act as a sort of lock, holding the barriers between our world and others in place. She does this by offering herself up to the Outer Gods themselves, over and over again. The whole process is very esoteric.

"For the first time in recorded history, there is no Crimsonata. None that are flowing at least. The young woman who holds this title has no idea what she is or what she is supposed to do. If Audrey Lynn Darrow does not flow, the barrier between our world and the others will shatter. The earth will be torn asunder as the multiverse collapses in upon us."

Hayden sneered. "It all sounds like foul magic work. Why not just kill this Darrow woman?"

"Because then there will absolutely be no lock for the barrier and our world is doomed."

"What do you expect us to do?" asked Roma. "The Wall isn't exactly in the habit of helping the supernatural."

Faure sighed. "Darrow must be found and captured. She must be forced to flow, even if that means against her will. This is for the greater good."

Roma looked disgusted but said nothing. Greer lit up a cigarette and shrugged. Faure glanced at Hayden, but the large man merely glowered at him.

"Listen, I can give you whatever details you need along with my contact information. And the contact information for Professor Binici. She's part of the Wall and part of this, too. She knows more about the Crimsonata than anyone else. Once you've secured Darrow, she'll be meeting up with you."

"The Promethean Wall have contacts across the entire planet, in every branch of the military and law enforcement. We know how to do our fucking jobs."

"Alec, clam down," said Roma, looking over at Hayden. "This is a little outside our wheelhouse, and it sounds big. There are just as many brains as there as fists in the Wall."

Hayden stormed off muttering under his breath, but Faure wasn't sorry to see him go. The man seemed like a loose cannon, someone who brought his own prejudices into a mission. He hoped Roma could keep him contained. The Darrow woman absolutely couldn't be harmed – the state of their reality depended on it.

It pained him to think that he had basically sanctioned kidnapping and then forcing a young woman into what amounted to slavery. Is that what it was like for the Crimsonata when she flowed? He had no idea. Even Binici wasn't entirely sure, but that uncertainty was not going to be enough to make him divert from his course.

"Okay," said Faure. "What do you need from me?"

CHAPTER 13

Elliot was trying to cheer Audrey up, but it wasn't working very well. Driving along, he had spied a carnival and stopped. She hadn't wanted to go, but felt bad telling him no. Instead, she let him drag her into the crowd, her anxiety winding itself tighter. She could feel it racing along her skin, her nerves electric.

Jittery, she tried not to think about all of the people around her. Loud and moving, a mass of humanity shambling about her. Grabbing Elliot, she hauled him over to a stand and made him buy her a lemon shake. She wished it was half filled with vodka. The stand next to it was selling funnel cakes and Elliot bought one of those, too. Audrey slurped on her drink and picked at the powdered sugar topped treat, trying to feel normal.

Some girls around her age, probably a little younger, walked by. She caught her brother checking them out and smiled. All three of them were attractive, clad in shorts and tank tops. She could be one of them, but she wasn't. She never had been. Too weird, too dark, too distant. Even the people she called friends she knew weren't really friends by normal standards. Those same people likely considered her just an acquaintance.

She hated feeling this way. Some days were worse than others, sure, but it was always there. The sadness, the fear, the emptiness. The anxiety and depression spinning in a vicious cycle, with paranoia as sprinkles on top. Closing her eyes, Audrey tried to shut everything out, only for a few moments, just to center herself.

"You okay?" asked Elliot.

"I'm fine," mumbled Audrey.

"We can leave," his said, concern in his voice.

"I'm fine," she replied, opening her eyes.

Across the midway, standing beside the ring toss, was the man in the suit.

He was smiling at her.

The breath caught in Audrey's throat. She grabbed at Elliot's arm, almost making him drop the funnel cake. People continued waking through the midway, and in those few seconds, he was gone.

"What's wrong?"

"I thought... nothing."

Everything jumped out at her now, everything was menacing. She wasn't even aware of Elliot leading her back through the carnival, back to the car. Too much was happening around her, too much threatened her. Carnies shouted madness while children ran screaming past her. Old people loitered in the middle of the thoroughfare while teenagers made out behind concession stands. A slice of pizza fell to the ground uneaten and balloons slipped away into the sky. Poorly played country music was performed on a rickety stage and trashcans overflowed. A line formed by the port-a-potties and the tilt-a-whirl spun out delighted shrieks.

A little boy ran into Audrey and she screamed.

The boy jumped back, equally scared. His mother ran over, protective and glaring at Audrey. She led the boy away as Audrey clutched onto her brother, unable to move.

"Come on, we're almost out of here," he said.

She followed him the rest of the way to the car, trying to ignore the chaos around her. She tried not to think about seeing the man in the suit again and what that could mean. She'd never hallucinated before and it terrified her to go down that line of thought. She remembered enough of her mother, that madness, and had always feared it would come looking for her.

Collapsing in the car, she couldn't keep the tears at bay any longer. Breaking down in front of Elliot, letting him see her this way, made her cry even harder. He deserved better. He deserved a better sister than she could give him.

Expecting pity or even disgust, she instead found his arms around her, hugging her tight.

"I am so, so sorry," he said. "I shouldn't have brought us here, I shouldn't be trying so hard. Whatever you need, okay?"

Audrey cried a little longer, her emotions trying to stabilize. After a bit, she pulled herself from her brother's arms and sniffed. "I'm sorry, I got snot all over your shirt."

"Have you met me? I get grosser shit than that on me when I eat."

Audrey let out a little laugh. "And I'm sorry for getting like that."

"It happens. It's okay."

"No, it's really not."

Elliot frowned. "Audrey, you're my sister, and I love you. Get used to it."

She not tried to start crying again. It was strange to not be alone, strange to know there was someone out there who loved her. Family. She simply wanted to be worthy of that love. She wished she could explain that to Elliot.

It occurred to her that she did love Elliot. She had never really thought about it before. He was a good person, a better person than her. He was her brother, half or not. She would finish this trip for him, no matter what.

"Can we go back to the motel?" she asked.

"Sure, if that's what you want."

"I want to rest. No, I want to get drunk. Please? I want to sit in some air conditioning, drink too much cheap booze, and relax with my baby brother."

"I can ensure that happens," said Elliot with a smile. "Any choice of cheap booze?"

Audrey turned on the stereo as Elliot pulled the car out of the parking lot. Lana Del Rey played as dust kicked up behind them. She lit up a cigarette and sighed.

"Get a gallon of crap lemonade and a fifth of gas station vodka. We're drinking ghetto tonight."

CHAPTER 14

The famed mythologist Joseph Campbell said *Every religion is true one way or another. It is true when understood metaphorically.* Professor Binici cared very little about faith, only about the facts buried beneath. The cultures that practiced these ancient beliefs were more interesting to her than the beliefs themselves. She left the stargazing to colleagues like Timothy Faure.

The summer was supposed to be spent working on another book, her first that would make veiled connections to the Crimsonata. After two years, it still didn't feel anywhere near finished. Binici knew she would be lying to herself if she said that she didn't hope the Wall found Audrey Darrow for her own personal gain. She had too many questions that a library of books simply couldn't answer.

So many things nagged at her that she hoped Darrow could answer. How often did she have to perform the ritual and how long did it last? Would the process be visible to outside observers? Did blood truly flow out of her? What was the sensation like? So much could be tied together from all her years of research, speculations finally laid to rest.

Binici took another bite of her sandwich and placed it back on the paper plate sitting on the edge of her desk. Most of the desktop was taken up by books and paper. The sun was setting outside, but she had flipped on the two bright floor lamps an hour ago. Across from her on the wall hung a print of *Ophelia by the Water* by J.W. Waterhouse, one of her favorite artists. She stared at it while she took another bite of her sandwich, trying to clear her head.

There was so much information out there and it had proven difficult to discern what was relevant and what wasn't.

She was reasonably sure that while The Venus of Willendorf was an ancient symbol of the Scared Feminine, it didn't tie into the Crimsonata. She wasn't as sure about all of the supposed Grail Lore, although so much of it was conjecture. How did Mother Mary, or for that matter Mary Magdalene, factor in? From what Binici had deduced, the Crimsonata were exclusively a line of women. Could that have played a role in what was considered the historical Jesus's remarkable birth? Perhaps it was all unrelated. The word "ritual" came from "rtu," the Sanskrit word for menses, but that didn't mean everything was linked.

Binici had found fragments of texts that tied her research to the Roma Gypsies and Greek Oracles, Druid Clans and Persian Scholars. An entire African Tribe had been built around their "Bleeding Chieftess" for generations until they were wiped out by a neighboring tribe. There were thousands of notations on wise women, priestesses, witches, and even queens, all of whom were considered magical due to something about their blood. Something about it that was different, that granted abilities.

The books Faure provided had been illuminating. Outside of the most basic historical texts, and their uncertainty, lay the superstitions. Often based on some type of truth, Binici found a host of things to ponder there.

Vampires she dismissed outright but found much of the conflicting stories fascinating. She read about the Egyptian goddess Isis and the Mayan goddess Ixchel, then about Lilith. While none of these specifically recalled Crimsonata lore, Binici could see where things could have been twisted. Aswang, Succubus, Harpy. She found it most interesting that the female Furies of Greek myth were birthed when drops of Titan blood fell upon the earth.

So much of that research took her back to superstitions concerning the menstrual cycle and Binici wanted to stay away from that. Not only had that line of academia already been thoroughly studied, it had very little bearing on the Crimsonata. At least as far as she knew. Everything pointed at the Crimsonata being about lineage, station, and ability. She had a grasp on the first two.

There used to be more than one Crimsonata, probably dozens. Although the world's population had exploded, the Crimsonata's numbers had dwindled. A patriarchal world society probably had something to do with that, plus a tightening of religious fundamentals in regions where religion wasn't just simply dying out. There was no place in the world for them anymore. In the last two centuries, they had likely gone about their practices in secret, ostracized from the rest of their respective societies. Binici also guessed that many died without giving birth to an heir.

The Promethean Wall hadn't even been aware of the Crimsonata until she brought the matter to them. When she spoke to the gentleman in Washington DC, he hadn't seemed terribly concerned. Audrey Darrow was the last of her line, not even aware of what she was. That had been years ago. They had agreed to help her seek out what little information they could for her research on the condition that she keep them informed on any changes with Darrow.

Audrey didn't know that Binici had been watching her for years.

Binici felt for the sad, lost young woman. There had been many times she wanted to break her silence and go to Audrey, to tell her everything. Perhaps that would've been for the best. Binici had played that conversation over and over in her head countless times, but it had never ended well. She hated that things were taking such a dark turn now, but part of her felt like they were always destined to go this way.

Her sandwich forgotten, she tried not to think back to that night in San Diego when she had officially joined the Wall. They had taken her to a warehouse and showed her something that had been birthed into this world through unnatural means.

It lunged at the bars of its cage, thick mucus flung from its tentacles and splattered on the floor. Squeals, shrills and loud, had echoed throughout the building. The nightmare had a slobbering mouth at the center of its mass, rows and rows of tiny needle teeth. She was made to watch as they killed the horror, setting upon it with a flamethrower. She was made to watch so that she knew exactly what the Wall was up against.

That had been just one, one of many waiting to get in.

It was why Audrey had to flow.

CHAPTER 15

The booze had been procured and drank, and for a short period of time, Audrey felt at ease. Yes, the alcohol had helped, but Elliot was the main contributing factor. They had just lounged around the motel room and hung out, talking and laughing. He had laughingly sprayed a mouthful of chips across the room during her rant about Princess Leia. Audrey felt that as a twin, Leia should be featured as more of a Jedi badass like her brother. In her drunken state, she had made this impassioned argument full of cursing. As both a feminist and a geek, too, Elliot had to laughingly agree.

She let loose with her movie trivia, regaling her brother with countless tidbits of information concerning science fiction and horror movies. They talked over the merit of sequels, the dubious need of reboots, and the how neither of them were purists when it came to book adaptations. Elliot was far more into horror movies than she was, she more into comic books, but they agreed on a ton on stuff. *Twilight* fans were worse than the books, Ripley was the greatest heroine to ever grace the screen, and the loss of *Firefly* was a national tragedy.

Elliot had passed out on the bed, face down on the comforter. Fortunately he had taken off his shoes hours ago. Audrey was exhausted but worried she wouldn't be able to sleep. Worse, she worried that her brain would keep spinning while she laid there, dragging her back to dark places. Flipping off the lights, she unfastened her bra and pulled it out from underneath her tank top. She slid off her shorts and climbed into her bed, hoping she could find slumber under the sheets.

Surprisingly, it came quickly.

Unfortunately, things were waiting for her.

Audrey found herself on a hardwood floor, dressed as she had been in bed. Clad only in white underwear and a green ribbed tank top, she climbed to her feet. The room was dark and smelled horribly, like a cross between spoiled meat and burnt motor oil. The air was thick, humid, and there was some type of haze. She could make out a faint light and walked toward it on bare feet.

Another room, and then another. Weak light seeped in from cracks in the doors, promising other exits, but the doors wouldn't open. In the third room, Audrey stopped. She wasn't alone in the room. Something stood silent, motionless in the corner. No words would come to her, fear trapping them inside. There was a shuffling, like cloth against cloth. Whoever it was turned and exited through a door that hadn't been there previously. Compelled, Audrey followed.

This new room was bigger than the others from what she could tell, the ceiling higher, but the haze thicker. The gloom threatened to envelop her, and Audrey began to back up the way she came. The door she had entered by was gone. She slapped her hands on the wall in a futile attempt to make it reemerge. Spinning back around, she found shapes drifting out of the miasma. Five, ten, dozens. They all looked like the mad woman who had attacked her and Elliot at the casino — men and women dressed in white rags, their faces sliced apart, and their fingers ending in claws.

None of them lunged at her or said a thing, as had the other from before. They moved slowly, deliberately. They came at her from the sides and began to encircle her, keeping a wide breadth in the center. They were herding her. Audrey was forced away from the wall and deeper into the room.

To her left, she saw a lattice-work of metal reaching to the ceiling. Men and women hung naked from it, many weeping quietly. They didn't seem to notice her. A massive block of meat stood in the center of the room, glistening with oils. Behind it in the darkness, even darker shadows still shifted. *Whatever they were looked to be immense and inhuman. She thought she caught the reflection of eyes peering down at her.*

Nearing the back of the room, the circle began to thin out, leaving room for Audrey to see a stage. On it sat two chairs that appeared to be composed of some tar-like material that had hardened, as if they had exploded out of the ground in that shape and set. Two figures in black robes were seated on them, examining her as she was brought before them.

"So you are the Crimsonata," spoke one of them.

"The jailer who would deny us our right," said the other.

Audrey was trapped under their gaze, red embers that burned beneath their hoods. She had no idea what was happening, what they meant. This couldn't be real, but it felt like more than just a nightmare. She held up her hands, her reason still abandoning her.

"Pitifully human," one said. "And we thought she would be a threat."

"Not to the Ovessa. Not to our great glory."

Together they gestured toward the ceiling and Audrey looked up. For a moment, all she saw was haze, but then it parted. It parted, and there was something more. Writhing and thrusting, it sat floors above. Hating and lusting, it wasn't occupying any actual space, but existed between spaces. Ready to come through. A star of flesh, its grey luminosity filtering down to shine throughout the building. A perversity of natural order, the entity exuded sadism and control. It had risen up, so it could reign above.

Audrey saw all this, knew all this, and began to scream.

She screamed so hard she almost threw herself from the bed.

For a split second, she thought she saw the man in the suit standing there in her room. She blinked, and he was gone. Elliot wasn't though, having been awakened by her scream. He fumbled off his bed, looking around, confused and ready to fight. But the monsters were gone, banished from her head.

Audrey collapsed back onto her bed, sweat soaked through her tank top. Terrified, she tried to piece together what had just happened to her. Something more than a nightmare? Either way, the question that worried her the most – what was happening to her?

CHAPTER 16

Everybody joined the Promethean Wall for different reasons.

Allison Roma had joined because of her sister. Her older sister had been murdered by a serial killer in the late 1990's, one who was collecting pieces of young girls for a ritual. They had eventually found the killer, dead in his home. Mysterious circumstances. That had never sat right with Roma and she spent her life investigating it. Eventually she stumbled upon the Wall, and through them, the answer. It turned out that the killer had actually completed his ritual, at which point the extra-dimensional creature it summoned had simply drained him of life and went back home. The Wall had confiscated all of the arcane texts.

The Wall was everywhere. While not an officially sanctioned branch of the government, they had members and allies in all levels of all offices. It was believed that while no President had any direct knowledge of the Wall, so that he could claim plausible deniability, all except one in the past fifty years had been quietly supportive. The same could be said of the heads of state in over thirty countries around the world.

Private individuals and corporations, as well as governments, provided resources and funds to the Wall. Safe houses needed to be kept up, individual cells provided with a stipend. Vehicles, weapons, computers, and other necessities were always seen to. Members had access to everything from law enforcement data to mystical grimoires. Whatever was needed.

The mission statement was simple – protect humanity from supernatural interference. Some cells interpreted this statement differently than others. Some cells openly employed the use of arcane warfare themselves, while others found any taint of the metaphysical to be deplorable. Hayden ran his cell like the latter.

Roma didn't know what had brought Hayden to the Wall. His hatred of the supernatural was almost pathological. She didn't know much about him at all, other than that he had a high close rate. She had been living in Virginia before joining him here.

Greer had been a cop once; that much she knew. Something had happened while he was on the force that had led him here. He didn't say much, and Roma was okay with that. She got the impression that some of Hayden's ideals didn't sit too well with Greer either.

"Now we know why that took so long," said Hayden, coming into the room.

"What's up?" asked Roma.

"The Crimsonata isn't at her home, she's on a road trip with her half-brother, Elliot Byrnes. They're in Mississippi. Last used his credit card at a motel."

Roma frowned. "There're at least twenty cells closer than us. Why are we doing this?"

"Because we were tasked with it."

Roma didn't like that answer. She remembered how Hayden had reacted to Faure's story concerning the girl. She was innocent in all of this, but he viewed her as another monster.

"How sure are we about this intel?" asked Roma. "As I recall, you had a hard time swallowing it."

"Faure and that Binici he mentioned are both in good standing with the Wall. They're both just brains, but they've put in the years. I have to take their assessment as credible. You were the one who was inclined to believe, as I remember it."

"I'm just asking questions, Hayden."

He didn't say anything and started packing up gear. She watched as he loaded two Uzis into a case and sighed silently to herself. She harbored misgivings about this cell assignment since the day she arrived. Greer was alright by himself, she could handle his attitude, but it was difficult when paired with Hayden. Hayden was always on, always militant. She wondered how things had worked in his last Cell but knew it would be pointless to ask – he would just blow off the question.

Roma hadn't wanted to leave Virginia, but the cell was getting too large. As the seventh and newest member, she had to be transferred when an older member had returned from an extended European mission. She had been given a few choices and had picked Indianapolis at random. Even now, she could request a transfer out, the higher ups could see to that, but she didn't want to rock the boat.

Hayden dropped three pairs of handcuffs into a bag and Roma shook her head. She didn't feel good about this mission. It wasn't even the whole supposed fate of the world mumbo-jumbo that Faure had told them, it was the logistics. Kidnapping some girl who was only a little bit younger than her wasn't what the Wall did. And how were they supposed to make her do this magic act? Roma didn't like to think about what Hayden had in store for Audrey Darrow if she refused him. The more she thought about the whole thing, the more it sickened her.

Greer came back into the house and threw the keys on the table. The SUV was gassed up. She still had to pack and get her gear ready. Leaving the other two, she went upstairs to the bathroom. It was mostly her stuff in there and she picked up her hair brush, deodorant, and a few other items. Carrying them to her room, she dropped them on her bed and pulled her long, thick, black hair back into a ponytail. Into a suitcase she quickly packed jeans, shorts, a few shirts, underwear, socks, bras, and her laptop.

Carrying it downstairs, she eyed her gear bag. It sat open, ready for guns, handcuffs, a Taser, a baton, knives, explosives, and various other tools of the trade. Sometimes it scared her how proficient she'd become in the use of all of these things.

But, she was a field operative for the Promethean Wall. This was the life she had chosen. She'd find Audrey Darrow and figure things out from there. She had already decided that she wouldn't let Hayden hurt the girl unless things absolutely had to go down that way. She knew where her line was, and she wouldn't be dragged across it by him.

Now she just had to remember where she put her extra ammo.

CHAPTER 17

Audrey sat at the picnic table and chain-smoked. They had checked out of the motel but not yet left, Elliot not ready to commit to the road. She knew he didn't want to proceed until she was ready, and she didn't know what she wanted to do. She hadn't been this bad in years. Her anxiety was through the roof, paranoia clawing at her. He was ready to pull the plug on the whole trip just for her.

Audrey had never been agoraphobic, but she had never been this far from home before either. She wondered if that had sparked everything, no sense of being stationary. She didn't think so, but she couldn't be sure.

It was actually pretty here. The parking lot in front of the motel butted up against a small wooded area, a few picnic tables nestled in among the trees. The light played down between the leaves, rustling in a slight breeze that cooled the sweltering temperature a bit. Someone had been feeding the wildlife, a pile of seeds sat nearby beneath another worn table. Audrey was making a pile of cigarette butts.

Elliot had run down the street to get food. She hadn't wanted to go with him, she just needed a moment to herself. Some silence and solitude. For a few brief moments she felt alright, at ease. The despair was scratching furiously at the doors, desperate to be let back in, but she lit another cigarette and stared off into the trees instead. She didn't turn when her brother pulled up behind her.

"They didn't have much. I got you a salad and mozzarella sticks."

"That's fine."

The salad was little more than iceberg lettuce with a few chunks of tomato and cucumber, but at least it was fresh. The mozzarella sticks were a perfect golden brown and pulled molten cheese out of each bite. Elliot dove into his giant pulled pork sandwich, napkins everywhere for the barbeque sauce. They ate in silence for a while, Audrey refusing to be the first one to speak.

Finally Elliot swallowed and looked up at her. "We can head back whenever you want to."

"I don't want to head back."

"You sure?"

"I don't *want* to head back, but I also want this to be fun for you."

"I am having fun," said Elliot.

"Yeah, in those few minutes when you're not worrying about me."

"Well, of course I'm going to worry about you."

"You shouldn't have to."

Taking another bite of cucumber, Audrey considered her choices. Even if they went back now, it would take them days to get home, even if they drove with minimal stops. Then she'd be returning to her small, meaningless life, one where she'd spiral into depression because she ended the trip early. Or she could power through it, possibly ruining the rest of the trip for Elliot as she likely continued her decline while they drew farther and farther away from home. Neither option seemed terribly appealing.

Reaching for another mozzarella stick, she glanced back toward the woods. She froze, her mouth open and the food halfway to it. Walking toward her out of the trees was the man in the suit.

He looked exactly as he did every time she had seen him, exactly as he had in the bar. Handsome, with short-cropped greying hair and stubble, an immaculate black suit and tie, grey shirt, and a red rose in his lapel. He strolled out of the woods with a smile on his face like everything was normal, as if he belonged there. The ninety-degree weather didn't seem to affect him in the slightest.

"Please tell me you see him," whispered Audrey.

"Yes," replied Elliot. "What the fuck?"

The man in the suit walked up to them and stopped, examining them at the picnic table with their meals. "This all looks quite pleasant."

"Who are you?" Elliot asked.

Audrey merely gawked at him, a combination of awe and terror.

"You can call me Mr. Inanis. It's a good enough name for this particular endeavor. By the looks on your faces, I'm guessing you both remember me."

"I've seen you," murmured Audrey.

"You were at the casino," said Elliot. "I saw you when that crazy woman attacked us. You vanished."

"I saved you from that, as you put it, crazy woman. I've been following you since then, in case they tried again."

"In case who tried again? What are you taking about?" asked Elliot, getting angry.

"Sorry Elliot Byrnes, you're irrelevant in all this. This is Audrey's story."

It felt like the gravity had shifted inside of Audrey, all the weight in her stomach dropping and her blood thinning out. Mr. Inanis caught her in his gaze and held it, the implications of his declaration pinning her to her seat.

"That was not just some crazy woman and you know it. It was a monstrosity, something once human, engineered into servitude to be the living extension of the will of something that this world has never seen. Using English terms, it's called an 'Invocated.' It was one of many, soon an army's worth."

Still no words could come from Audrey, none that mattered. Elliot spoke for her. "Why would it come after Audrey?"

"Because of who she is. Because of who her mother was, her grandmother, her great grandmother, and stretching back millennia. You are the last in the line of the Crimsonata."

"The what?" she managed to get out.

"The Crimsonata. A bloodline of women who possess unique abilities granted by remarkable blood. The Crimsonata engage in a ritual that allows them to flow. When the blood flows, as your kind has done for thousands of years, it feeds the Outer Gods and keeps them satiated. Satiated, they are satisfied to remain elsewhere, beyond this reality. Since you have not been seeing to your duties, they are restless."

"This is insane," said Elliot, getting up from the table.

Audrey held out her hand, gesturing for him to sit. "Tell me more."

"As the Outer Gods stir, the barriers built will start to crumble. Unfortunately, the first of those barriers to fall are the lowest. The denizens of the gutter realms have already stared to break through. Primitive gods and their puppets, which have existed beneath this universe, seething in contempt at their place in the cosmic scheme. They would see this reality assimilated or obliterated. This would be accomplished by killing you, putting an end to the Crimsonata line once and for all, freeing them forever."

"Audrey, you can't believe any of this?"

But she remembered her mother's words, remembered her mother locking herself away. She remembered piecing things together as a child, believing later that her mother was some kind of religious fanatic. She didn't remember everything, but she remembered enough. Enough to know that it fit, that it made sense.

Maybe she just wanted it to make sense. Maybe she wanted her mother to be more than just crazy and her life to have some meaning. It was insane, it was some story she would read or watch, now staring her. There was no reality where the rantings of her dead mother equaled this. But...

But part of her still believed.

"My mom died when I was seven," said Audrey. "I didn't know. I didn't... I don't know how to do any of this. I don't know if I even want to. What if I refuse?"

Mr. Inanis smiled. "Oh, well there are those who will try to force you to flow should you refuse. You should be aware of that. And the coming of the Outer Gods will most definitely annihilate this universe if it hasn't already been completely destroyed by the wars between all the other realms converging first."

"Jesus!"

"So right now, there are two factions on the hunt for you, one that wants to kill you and the other that wants to control you. That's exciting!"

Both Elliot and Audrey gaped at him, unable to process his enthusiasm.

"Which side are you on?" asked Elliot, sliding closer to his sister.

"Me? I'm an interested third party. You'll see me around."

The air shimmered like a wave of heat, but angular and flat. It rotated around Mr. Inanis, enveloping him. He disappeared before their eyes.

Elliot turned to Audrey. "So, um..."

Audrey began to cry.

CHAPTER 18

There is no singular answer, only fragments of a subjective truth. That truth, at its core, is what unifies humanity. That we exist, that we seek a place in this universe. It was the extraneous dressings that divided us and gave us the trappings of religion.

Perhaps an odd belief for a tenured professor of Comparative Religions, but Timothy Faure had always leaned more toward being an agnostic. He had studied so many of the world's faiths, he felt that he could not honestly choose one over another. Raised a blank slate by parents who were proto-hippies, he hadn't been burdened with any particular set of doctrines. His fascination with theology had come in college and it had been in an academic fashion.

It had stayed academic until several years ago when his studies led him to the Wall.

Faure was still unsettled by his meeting with the Wall. He worried about the success of the mission with someone like Hayden running the show. He would have reached out to someone else had he known that Dwight was dead, seeking council from someone directly in Washington, although his connection there was tenuous at best. The whole situation was delicate, and he hoped he hadn't made a mistake.

While there was still a late afternoon class on early Judeo-Christianity for him to teach, Faure cancelled it and left for home. There was too much buzzing in his head, too much pulling at his attention. He pulled into his driveway and saw his wife's car already parked. A sociology professor a few years older than him, they had an amicable if somewhat distant marriage of ten years. It worked for both of them.

Car parked in front of his ranch house, Faure grabbed his briefcase and went inside. Dorothy was at the small kitchen table that she used as desk, typing away, likely responding to emails. She smiled at his entrance.

"You're home early."

"I'm not feeling good. I think I'm going to the basement for a while."

He chose not to notice her barely concealed eye roll.

"That's fine dear."

Leaving his briefcase on the counter, he opened the door and descended the steps. The basement was mostly unfinished, filled with boxes, unused exercise equipment, Christmas decorations, and some old furniture they hadn't wanted to get rid of. A washer and dryer sat off to the side next to the water heater. In the far corner, a curtain had been hung to partition off a small section of the space. Faure undressed slowly, placing each item of clothing on a plastic chair, neatly folded. He breathed deeply as he continued the process, making it a ritual.

Stepping through the curtain, he entered the small shrine he had built years ago. Lighting incense, he examined all of the items he had assembled here. Tibetan prayer flags, Catholic crucifix, Norse rune stones, Taoist yin-yang, Wiccan pentacle, and a host other of religious iconography. While he did not believe in any of the items in and of themselves, he believed in the ideals they represented. The gestalt they could be. He had learned a greater truth thanks to the Wall. There was more, and he just had to be open to it.

Faure had devised his own ritual, one more in tune with psychology than with religion. The point was to realign his Super Ego, suspended on a Higher Plane. To further realize his archetype. Opening his mind to greater possibilities than this world, he attempted to calm his center.

Faure had no idea that something was waiting for him.

It wrapped around his mind with liquid coils, burrowing in. The scent of incense became putrid and oily, stinging his nose. It clung to his skin as he realized he wasn't in the basement anymore, he wasn't anywhere. The darkness around him was opaque, only broken by a haze that wavered and curled like cobwebs in the wind. Sweat poured from him, the abyss humid and filled with stagnant air.

He tried to find words, tried to find thoughts, but nothing came. Then a light began to shine, dull and cold, the aperture soft around the edges. It struck him whole, and Faure felt the perversity, the sadism in its glare. This was beyond anything he had ever studied in his meager books, something real and ready to make itself known. An engine of entropy that had ran for eons and would extinguish worlds, now became the engineer who had chosen to rebuild him with its radiant glance.

Faure understood. Through oppression came freedom. Freedom from the burden of free will, freedom from the burden of identity, freedom from the burden of choice. He longed for it, longed for the embrace of his new god. For the Ovessa. But it was still held back, too far away. The light began to dim, and Faure cried out, denied the touch.

He found himself back in his basement, the incense still smoking away. What had transpired had only taken moments. Only moments, but it had changed Faure irrevocably. There *was* a truth out there, one he'd never even been aware of. Faure realized he would do anything to touch the light of the Ovessa again. Its will was all that mattered.

Walking back upstairs, Faure forgot his clothes. He stepped into the kitchen naked and looked around. His wife peered up at him and squinted.

"What are you doing? Why are you naked?"

Faure stared at her for a second before pulling open a drawer and grabbing a steak knife. He lunged across the room, silent, but in his head the same three words played over and over.

For the Ovessa. For the Ovessa. For the Ovessa.

CHAPTER 19

Audrey leaned against the car and smoked another cigarette. To say she had no idea what to do would be an understatement. Paralyzed with indecision, she just kept smoking.

Part of her wanted to return home, take whatever was coming. Just face it, accept it. There was a certain relief in the idea of surrendering. But the more she thought about that, the more it pissed her off. She hadn't asked for this, for a mother getting killed before passing down some bullshit arcane secrets to her. Her life hadn't exactly been easy. She resented what was being asked of her.

Did she believe everything Mr. Inanis had said? Maybe? Yes? She didn't know. Not only did it fit with what little she remembered about her mom, it fit with the hole she felt in her life. Of course she was supernatural being with magical blood that saved the world – as if she didn't have enough anxiety in her life. Always something wrong, always something to be paranoid about. This would explain why, she felt. In some ways it was liberating, this knowledge. Mostly it was terrifying. Maybe she was as crazy as her mother

She had borrowed Elliot's penknife and made a tiny cut along the tip of her middle finger. He'd been pissed, but she ignored him. Audrey had stared at the bit of blood that welled up, wondering what all the fuss was about. A normal reddish color, it certainly didn't glow or display any super powers. She sucked on her finger, wondering about these other people who Mr. Inanis said were searching for her, those he said would force her to use her abilities. Good luck with that.

"We can't just sit here, Audrey."

She nodded, barely hearing her brother. What would it mean to use her powers? Would she go crazy as she remembered her mom, or was that just her mom? Would her whole life become dedicated to it? She knew her mom had a job, but she couldn't recall what it was. Something menial. Audrey never wanted children, but would she be expected to carry on the line? Could she sentence a daughter to this life?

According to Mr. Inanis, if she didn't give in, the world could end. She found that somewhat hyperbolic, given that she was just a twenty-four-year-old web designer from northern California. Remarkably short, dry blonde hair pulled back in a ponytail, nails bitten down, bags under her eyes – she was all too human. She drew a line in the gravel with her shoe and examined her tanned leg. She hadn't even shaved in days.

"Audrey, tell me what to do."

Two sides coming after her, one that wanted to kill her, the other that wanted to use her. God that pissed her off. It wasn't that Audrey was against exploring these supposed powers, but she wanted it to be on her own terms. And she was pretty against the idea of anybody killing her. The whole situation made her want to scream and hide, but she knew she couldn't do that. This wasn't going away.

Then there was Elliot. He wasn't going to leave her side. She had to factor him into everything. What would be the best for *them?* Audrey lit up another cigarette and stared out into the trees.

* * *

Elliot paced back and forth on the other side of the car as Audrey chain-smoked and gazed off into the distance. He understood that she had to process everything that vanishing weirdo had told her, but they had to move. If even half of what he said was true, they weren't safe staying here any longer. She really needed to process these thoughts on the road.

He knew that he was just pissed because he didn't know how to protect her from this. His sister was fragile, and he'd sworn to himself that he'd always be there for her, be there for her now because he'd hadn't been able to be in the past. But this was all new, this was something entirely different. This was magic and monsters, and Elliot felt helpless. He couldn't imagine how Audrey felt, caught in the middle of it.

In his opinion, their best option was just to run. They still had a ton of money and they could make it last for quite a while. Learn all they could about what was going on and find a way around it. Elliot was an optimist and always thought there was a better way, another way out. He'd figure it out, save his sister.

That Inanis guy had thrown him. Elliot may have loved his comic books and sci-fi movies, but he never expected to see a guy disappear like that after dropping tales about cosmic gods and magic bloodlines. Part of him was excited by it, and he hated that part of himself, knowing that Audrey was in danger because of it. He wished she would just talk to him, in the car and on the move, so he could calm down.

At that thought, Audrey flicked her spent cigarette butt across the gravel and climbed into the car, Elliot scrambling into the driver's side. He turned the engine as she found Alkaline Trio on the stereo and cranked it up. Peeling out of the motel parking lot, he turned to her, eyebrow raised.

"We're on a road trip," she said. "Let's go."

"You're serious?"

"I can either turn myself over to them easily back home or make it hard for them. All of them. And if I use these powers of mine, even if they are real, it's going to be because I choose to use them, not because I was forced to."

"I support that."

"So fuck it, on to the next state."

Elliot said nothing for a minute, the sounds of the punk band roaring through the speakers.

"I'll stand beside you through all of it," said Elliot. "I need you to know that."

"I know," said Audrey, quietly. "Thank you."

CHAPTER 20

Southard, Indiana was a small town that had fallen on hard times. Never a booming metropolis, once the dog food plant and the textile mill had closed, the economy had all but dried up. Nothing remained for the struggling few thousand residents, nothing but desperation and empty promises.

For Sale signs marked houses like gravestones, a ghost town in the making. Most had an asking price that was ridiculously above market value in a town that offered nothing, people hoping to make enough to start again elsewhere. The few that had reasonable prices were in various states of disrepair or in undesirable locations. Even those who wanted to flee Southard found it hard to escape.

Most of Main Street found itself boarded up, the shops along the street closed down. No more butcher shop or pet store, no more coffee shop or office supply store. The beauty salon had cut back its hours next to the empty dollar store, the police no longer calling on half the bars whose doors were now permanently closed. Even the churches felt the sting, the good white Protestants no longer having the money to pay their tithe.

Without the taxes, the city itself soon fell into disrepair. The roads were pock-marked with potholes, left unattended to crack and grow worse. Unplowed and unsalted in the winter, they were treacherous. In the summer, like now, they expanded and cracked even more. Weeds sprouted up among municipal sidewalks and litter was left scattered everywhere. This said nothing of the police and fire departments who were severely cut back to skeleton crews each shift, barely able to deal with the growing unrest that claimed the town.

Southard was falling apart, falling in on itself. Those who could run already had, and those who couldn't were furious at their fate. The decay of the town was evident everywhere you looked, in every ruined building and every vacant parking lot, in every mangy stray cat and every yellowed clump of weeds. In every seething face of its citizens.

But this day, quietly, in the shadows inside the abandoned dollar store, things changed.

A cold, dull light blossomed, a light that illuminated nothing. It opened wider, deeper, and a door split open. Two figures in black cloaks came striding through and surveyed the space. It was a big room, one that would accommodate. One of the figures gestured and others began stepping through.

The room filled with beings that looked similar to each other. Their faces mutilated, their lips, noses, eyelids, ears, and hair hacked off, they all wore their wounds proudly. Fervently. Their bodies were adorned in white rags, covering flesh that was sweating with a sticky, moist substance. Parts of that flesh had been replaced with foreign matter, something more akin to a fungus, something that now throbbed in unison with their original meat. Their fingertips had been whittled down to expose sharpened bone.

Over one hundred of the Invocated swayed back and forth under the will of the Spittle and the Sigh.

Southard thought it knew despair, believed it had hit rock bottom. The Reverend of the Methodist church preached from his pulpit about hope while drinking himself into oblivion most evenings. The mayor, who had only won by a slight margin, had only ran for office to further his own petty, political career and couldn't wait until his term was up so that he could move on to better things. The only remaining member of what laughingly called itself the Chamber of Commerce took his rage out on his family every night. A teenage girl, who had been one of that year's high school valedictorians, had discovered that she was pregnant and saw her life slipping away. A junkie owed his dealer over five hundred dollars from a bungled meth deal and assumed he'd be dead in a week. A father hasn't had a job in three weeks and does not have the willpower to tell his family. An old woman lay dying of cancer and can't wait for it to finally take her so that she can be with her husband. A nurse at a clinic has been stealing pain meds for her back, and knows she must stop before she's caught, but she's addicted.

This is life, this is Southard.

But not for much longer.

The Spittle and the Sigh give the Invocated their orders, tell them to wait until nightfall. Tell them to be swift and to be silent. This is to be the first announcement, a declaration of intent. The Ovessa wills it so.

This was a good town once. Once it prospered and was filled with people who had happiness. People who worked hard, were friendly to their neighbors, and looked forward to tomorrow. Average people, but people with love and family and dreams, none the less. That was taken from them by a greed that was far more powerful than them. But they still had their lives. They still, perhaps somewhere buried deep down, had a seed of hope.

But the light of the Ovessa would see that seed burnt away under its might, Southard used for its glory. All will wither under its radiance, either culled or repurposed. But before that, some will become harbingers, heralds to the babbling meat of what is to come. Let them all be aware so that they will accept the Ovessa on their knees as proper supplicants, let them be in awe so that they will beg the Ovessa for its blessing as an Invocated.

The Spittle and the Sigh have watched this world through the barrier with disgust for centuries, ever since the Ovessa created them for that very purpose. They revel in the thought of consuming it, of conforming it to the will of the Ovessa. In their own realm, only they are burdened with the hideousness of identity, of uniqueness. But they exist to serve their Most Holy. Through their actions, Its will is made manifest.

Standing by the undulating dull light, the Spittle gestures to allow the Sigh entry back through the doorway first. She returns to the place they had first claimed in this world, and the Spittle glances around at the horde poised to strike later that night. A smile pulls at the cartilage and bone that makes up his face.

"All in honor of the Ovessa."

CHAPTER 21

Roma could tell that the motel manager's whiney, dismissive voice was pissing off Hayden. The rotund man shuffled around behind his desk, wheezing and swatting at flies. He wasn't being very cooperative. It was apparent that Hayden was ready to reach across the desk and bash the manager's head off the fading, cracked countertop multiple times until he got the answer he wanted.

Trying a different tactic, Roma unbuttoned the rest of her polo top and leaned over the counter. She tapped her nails slowly, getting the man's attention. A few choice words about the heat drew his eyes straight to her cleavage.

"I really wanted to see my friend Audrey, ya know. Like, meet up? My boyfriend and I were gonna meet her and her brother Elliot for some fun. I hope they haven't left, mister. I was reaaally looking forward to it."

The manager stumbled and blurted something out about the Byrnes kid checking out with a hot blonde hours ago. That was his sister? Poor bastard.

They were out the door before he could ask them if they wanted a room.

Re-buttoning her shirt, Roma glanced around and spied Greer beside the parking lot, near a picnic table. She headed toward him, Hayden following. She was worried about their cell leader, he hadn't been this edgy since they took down that Rathook cult in Wisconsin.

That had been bad. A group of PTA soccer moms had discovered a forgotten Chthonic goddess that offered them eternal youth and endless power in return for virginal sacrifices. It was like something out of a bad television show, except young girls were actually going missing in the small town. The FBI had initially thought a sexual predator or a serial killer was on the loose, but a Promethean Wall ally had contacted them, feeling it could be something worse.

It had taken three weeks to track them down in the basement of a white, Tudor-style home. Six women, who should have been between the ages of forty-nine and thirty-seven, all who looked barely thirty now. Women who had kidnapped another fourteen-year-old girl, while the Wall had been in town and helpless to save her, her body never recovered. They had found the women with yet another fifteen-year-old in the basement, their latest acquisition, naked and bound to the floor. Something slithered and oozed in the corners of the room, lit only by candles. It squealed when the Wall put bullets into the heads of all six women and retreated back into whatever shadowy depth it had crawled out of.

They had untied the girl, made sure she was alright, turned on the lights, and left. The police had connected the dots as they saw fit with the gun dropped beside one of the bodies. It was all covered up neatly. No one wanted to know the truth.

Roma wasn't sure she wanted the truth now. She had a feeling it would be way too complicated.

"They were here," said Greer, looking toward the table. "For a while, too. There in the parking lot as well. Intel says this is the brand she smokes. The bits of tobacco stuck near the filter are still dry in the grass, no dust on the butts in the lot. We just missed them."

Roma nodded. "Jives with what the manager said."

"We need to be in front of them," said Hayden, pulling out his phone.

"What are you doing?"

Hayden didn't answer and instead turned away from her. With a sigh, Roma wondered about their options. In an emergency case, they could call in favors and get an APB called out on someone, but that was usually on someone they could just kill and then blame on circumstances. They still didn't know where they were supposed to take this chick once they kidnapped her, or even how to get her away from her brother. Roma worried that Hayden already had ideas about that.

"Damn it," said Hayden, hanging up.

"What?"

"Tried calling Faure, but no answer."

"Try calling that Binici professor."

"I don't know her. I only will if I have to."

Greer shrugged. "We stay in the car like the time we were tracking that Changeling Killer in Iowa."

Hayden raised an eyebrow at him and Roma groaned.

"It worked, didn't it?"

It had. The Changeling kept killing people every two or three days, men and women. It ate a portion of their bodies and then used that genetic material to transform into them. Wearing their clothes, using their car and whatever possessions they had on them, it would then live as it saw fit for a few days until it found a new victim. The Wall kept racing behind it, fumbling over bodies. It took them a while to realize it was always using its newest victim's credit cards. Using the Wall's resources, they waited until another body dropped and then sought out any activity on that victim's cards. They had found the dead man's lookalike drinking champagne in a strip club in downtown Des Moines.

"Why go east when they may have gone north, let's just wait," said Roma.

"You're in charge of the laptop, keep it open and ready," Hayden said to her.

"Fine, but I get the backseat then."

"Whatever."

Roma paused. "Have you thought about what you plan on doing about the brother?"

"Nothing, as long as he doesn't get in our way."

"It's her brother, Alec."

"Then I'll probably have to put him down."

She didn't say anything as she walked back. It was her own fault for asking. She didn't want to know the truth, but now she did.

CHAPTER 22

The blood was everywhere. Dripping off the table, smeared on the walls, pooling on the floor. There was a time when this would have bothered Timothy Faure, but not now. Now it was simply red against white, an effect of his actions.

The microwave beeped, and he opened the door. A few chunks of his wife lay steaming inside. A few pieces of leg, a lower lip, some random organ he had pulled out. He decided he wanted to know what she tasted like cooked. Reaching in, he pulled out the mangled piece of lip, curled and greyed, and popped it in his mouth. It had lost much of its flavor, drying out too much. The piece of leg was much better.

Strolling across the kitchen, he kicked his butchered wife's corpse out of the way and sat down at the table, chewing on her flesh. Decisions had to be made. He'd seen the face of the divine had now had to act accordingly. The Ovessa must be freed.

Information had been given to him, seared into his mind. He could feel the Most Holy trying to reach through the barrier from where it sat. That he would run to the Ovessa was a given, but other matters had to be dealt with first. Stopping the Promethean Wall was of the utmost importance. They couldn't be allowed to get their hands on the Crimsonata, not when she held the ability to deny the Ovessa its right to this world.

Faure went to his briefcase and got out his phone, pacing a call to Binici. She didn't pick up and he didn't leave a voice mail. He left the phone on the counter and went upstairs to shower the blood from himself.

He didn't think about his wife's cooling body in the kitchen, didn't regret his actions. None of it mattered. The thought had simply crossed his mind and he acted upon it. Violence for the sake of violence. His wife had been nothing but animated meat, worthless in the greater cosmic scheme. Just like him. Just like all of humanity.

Washed and dried, he dressed only out of routine and because he would arouse suspicion if he engaged in his activities naked. He packed no additional clothing, took nothing except what was needed to achieve his goals. Wallet, keys, glasses, the items he wore. Faure went back downstairs, confident in his purpose.

He rang Binici again, this time getting an answer.

"Timothy, is everything alright?"

"No, the Crimsonata has been eluding the Wall. It's believed she knows she's being pursued, and we'll have better luck if you bring her in."

"What? That was never discussed."

"A change of tactics. They want you to handle it and then bring her to Eldridge, Ohio for containment. They have the most appropriate safe house there to accommodate her."

"Eldridge, Ohio?"

"I have no idea why, but yes."

"Timothy, I won't be able to get to any of this until tomorrow."

Faure sighed. "That's fine, but no later. We're on a clock here."

"If your people are sure..." Binici began.

"They are, Emily," Faure said, and then hung up before she could say anymore.

He slipped the cellphone into his pocket and walked back to the microwave. He took a bite out of the unknown organ, but it had gone cold. Unimpressed, he tossed it across the room. Surveying the atrocities, he considered setting fire to the house before deciding against it. It would bring people faster than just leaving everything as is. His wife wouldn't be missed for a few days, and chances were that by then, it would be too late for any human authorities to have a say in things.

Leaving the scene behind him, Faure walked out of his house and locked the door behind him. He climbed into his car and changed the music to Mozart. Pulling away, knowing he'd never see his home again, didn't shake him in the least. He was going to a new home, a new family. He was going to become a part of something bigger and grander, something that would usher in a new age upon the earth.

Idly, like one would consider the weather, Faure thought about all of the billions who prostrated themselves in the name of false faiths across the globe. It would be beautiful when they discovered the magnificent truth of the Ovessa and freed themselves from humanity's shackles. He knew he wasn't quite there yet, so close, but he wasn't invocated yet. A full transformation had yet to occur.

Faure knew he had been chosen because he was special, because he was in a unique position. Not only was he open to the call of the Ovessa, he was positioned to maneuver the Wall away from the Crimsonata so that the Ovessa's agents could strike. He was more than happy to be a pawn in his Most Holy's great will. For what the Ovessa had shown him, the majestic vistas of cosmic weight united under its shining rule, he would do anything to prove his devotion. Faure knew the Ovessa's plans culminated with the utter annihilation of the planet as earthlings knew it, terraformed into something far more primeval. It demanded that the spiritual eugenics of its populace merge into a singular, symbiotic lifeform, one that was both planet below and god above. All forever in the glistening glow of the Ovessa.

Yearning to touch that light again, Faure drove out of the city and headed east. He didn't know what he expected to find in Eldridge, but he would seek it out. He would do whatever was asked of him. Faure had studied enough religions to know what was expected of a devoted disciple, a loyal acolyte. He would prove his worth, no matter the cost.

Hitting the highway, he rolled down the window and turned up the music. Humming along with the tune, mile after mile passed, and he found himself smiling in anticipation.

CHAPTER 23

The motel was a single story, one-star shit hole right off the highway. Not that they had been staying in any terribly classy places on the trip, but this was the lowest on the totem pole so far. The carpet was so thread bare you could almost see the floor beneath and the peeling wallpaper was a salmon swirl that wasn't even in style back when it had been applied in the seventies. The particleboard end tables were chipped, and the brown woolen blankets frayed, the chances of bed bugs in the lumpy mattresses quite high. The curtains were plastic for some reason that Elliot couldn't figure out. The bathroom looked like a murder scene, hastily wiped down, and forgotten about. There was a rust tinge to everything in there.

At least there was air conditioning, a rickety contraption that made as much noise as it produced cold air. Elliot stood in front of it and considered sleeping on the floor that night. For the price he paid for the room, he was pretty sure it was mostly frequented by those not using the beds for sleep. But it was cheap, and he needed cheap right now. Who knows how long they'd be on the run.

He had suggested sleeping in the car, conserving money, but Audrey had shot him down. They'd worry about that when the money got thin, but not yet. He was more worried about when it got cold, if they could hold out for that long. They had already stopped off and got a case of cheap bottled water, and other cheap, nonperishable foods. Granola bars, trail mix, peperoni sticks, bags of baby carrots, snack crackers, jars of applesauce, etc. They would keep it all stored in the car just in case.

It was the unknown variables that kept Elliot twitching. Would this last a few days, a month, forever? He would stay with Audrey as long as it took, he owed her that, but he wished he knew what he was in for. For her part, after her initial freak out, she seemed to have found an equilibrium. A Zen with the whole thing. He didn't understand it, but he didn't really want to question it either. Elliot didn't like it when she cried.

Audrey was in the bathroom, cleaning up from the road. She had only brought her purse in, saying she'd change in the morning. He'd shrugged and gone along with her. Whatever she wanted to do, she was in charge.

To hell with it, thought Elliot, flopping down on top of the nearest bed. Back at school, he had been liked, popular among his circle. People gravitated to him, opened up to him. He had his crew of buddies that he had parties with, some he knew he'd stay friends with for years. While he had dated a decent amount, nobody had ever stood out to him. Most of the girls he met in college had either been husband hungry or party crazy, and he wasn't interested in either. He had never known any girls like his sister in school, and twice he had thought about asking her if she had any friends but decided that would be weird.

He had enjoyed college, and had enjoyed his major enough, but was more excited about the next chapter in his life than he was about the job. Elliot figured that was why he wasn't too freaked out about what was happening now. If he didn't get back in time, he'd just find another job. Whatever.

His mom barely understood what he did and had always given him a long leash as it was. She thought his devotion to a long-lost sister was odd, but she had never said a bad word. She had always known Audrey was out there, but never thought it was her place to say anything about it. A great mom, it tore Elliot up thinking how different Audrey might have been if she had been raised by her and their dad instead of spending all those years in foster care. Audrey said it was okay, but he tended to think otherwise.

He liked to think that his dad would be proud that Elliot was getting to know his sister, that they were together. And he didn't give a shit what Audrey's mom would've thought.

Audrey came out of the bathroom, her face washed, carrying her purse. She didn't wear a lot of makeup, just some eyeliner, shadow, sometimes blush, and bit of lip-gloss. Half the time, not even the last two. She popped off her sneakers and slid her bra out from underneath her shirt. Elliot smirked at a woman's ability to unfasten a bra clasp so effortlessly. Setting her purse at the foot of her bed, she slid the bra inside it, and set the shoes on top before dropping on top of the covers.

"I can feel the chlamydia fighting the gonorrhea to see who will crawl all over me," she said.

Elliot laughed. "I was thinking about sleeping on top of the covers, but that's probably just as bad."

"Probably."

She is so small, thought Elliot. The thought just struck him. She was as petite as that Lily girl he had dated. He had never really realized it. She had always seemed fragile, but never... small. She had a presence. In her own way, she was strong. She was her own person.

"You should get some sleep," said Elliot.

"You, too."

Elliot reached over and hit the light. Not for the first time, he wondered what it meant for Audrey to be the Crimsonata. If she chose that destiny, what her life would be. If she would even get that choice.

Maybe they should just turn north now. Head that way while they could. He was glad his car was only two years old and in great condition. Hit another state tomorrow. Tennessee? That sounded right. Wherever they needed to go.

Whatever Audrey needed.

CHAPTER 24

It was time for the will of the Ovessa to be imposed upon Southard, Indiana.

The Invocated slowly came out from their hiding place in the abandoned dollar store, under the cover darkness. The citizens had retreated to their homes, away from the failing businesses for the day, back to their small and miserable lives. The Invocated moved in droves, silent and swift, as the long reaching fingers of a greater intent.

They swept through the streets, gliding across asphalt and lawn alike. Clad in white, they were specters, wraiths, the personification of doom. Abominations lurched unheard toward doors and windows across the town, wiggled them open or broke them down, however they must. The noise woke some, but not many.

The Methodist Reverend was still so drunk he fell out of bed at the sound of his front door being bashed in. His mind couldn't process the noise he heard, couldn't even reconcile what time it was. He staggered from his bedroom, clad in underwear, T-shirt and one sock, to the top of his stairs and blinked bleary eyed down at the things rising up toward him. Without his glasses, he couldn't make out much. Dressed all in white, his fuzzy brain took them to be orderlies for a moment. But that didn't make sense. He opened his mouth to protest their presence in his home, only to find a hand thrust down his throat. It pushed him back as he felt fingers clawing apart his tongue. Flailing, he began to beat on the arm. Another hand found his neck and warm wetness spilled down the front of his shirt. The reverend called out for his god, but no answers came.

Looking over some late-night paperwork, the Mayor of Southard was wide-awake when the Invocated came crashing through the sliding screen door behind him. Screaming and pissing himself, he leapt up from his desk and tried to run to his gun cabinet. The creature swayed through the room, making its way towards him. Drawn by her husband's cries, his wife rushed down, only to be confronted by a monstrosity in white rags. Lunging, it gutted her with a single swipe. Still screaming, the Mayor continued to fumble with the lock on his gun cabinet as the Invocated bore down on him. Taking the Mayor's blubbering face in its hand, it began to carve haphazardly. Strips of skin fell in bloody tatters to the floor and continued to do so long after the Mayor had passed out.

The children of the man who ran the Chamber of Commerce hid in a closet and listened as the Invocated shattered their father's arms. In the dark, they could see nothing through the door but could hear all of it. They could hear their terrible, rage-fueled father whimper like an infant as more wet sounds were made. Wet, sloppy sounds. He whimpered and begged, his voice sounded like he had a mouthful of cereal. The children cowered and hugged onto each other, unable to imagine what could make their father sound like that. Then the closet door burst open and a nightmare stood over them, glaring down at them with eyes far too big. It would show them how such noises were made.

The high school valedictorian lay on her bed, bleeding out. She had been sound asleep when the attack came, barely conscious when the thing had gutted her. Her hand shaking, she tried to push her intestines back inside herself. No choice one way or another now, only death. She had heard her parents screaming shortly after waking, hadn't she? Maybe that had been her screaming. There had only been one incision, clean across her belly, dumping her out. The person who did it wore some kind of Halloween mask. She had no idea why, but it didn't matter now. She was so tired.

The meth junkie had been wide-awake, ready to leave his house to go to a friend's, and a hopeful score, when the

Invocated came. He ran, as fast and as far as he could. It hadn't helped. He had been found, crouched behind a dumpster blocks away, and cornered. At first the junkie tried to run again, a slash caught him in the ribs and he dropped to the street. Felled, three of the mutilated creatures surrounded him. He pleaded for his life, offering everything he could think of – money, drugs, sexual favors. The Invocated wanted nothing but to see the will of the Ovessa done. They tore into him, piece by piece, leaving little more than pulp and stain.

The father sobbed uncontrollably in his upstairs hallway, clinging to the body of his butchered wife. She'd bled out in his arms over ten minutes ago and there was nothing he could do about it. He was just as helpless to stop the maniacs from killing his three children, ages eleven, eight, and two. They had come in and laid waste to his family, laid waste to his life. What did a job matter when there was no one to take care of? The monsters hadn't touched him except to hurl him into the old wardrobe long enough to keep him out of the way. Seeing his whole family slaughtered was worse than dying. Did they know that, did they do that on purpose? He wept and held his cooling wife closer.

Gazing up at the Invocated from her recliner, the old woman simply said, "It's about time."

The nurse rushed down the hallway, chaos behind her. Something had overtaken the hospital, something butchering everyone in sight. There was blood everywhere, the smell of piss and feces pungent. Bodies lay where they had fallen. People dressed in white with faces out of a horror movie. The nurse found a scalpel on a forgotten surgical tray and hid in an empty patients' room. If she stayed behind the partition curtain, she thought she might be safe. Only moments later, the door was battered in and they swarmed. She screamed as they drug her to the floor and began their own procedure upon her. Bit by bit, her face was removed, pieces hurled against the window. Bit by bit, her sanity was drowned in blood.

Before dawn, the Invocated slunk back to the portal in the dollar store. Southard, Indiana has felt the First Announcement. It had a population of 8,924 and now it has far less. Only eighty-two of the Invocated were released on the town for a six-hour span, and in that time, over two-thirds of the town were either outright killed or grievously injured. Only a little over ten percent miraculously walked away without injuries of any kind, most of them seemingly sparred by the attackers for no reason.

It was too fast, too random, too chaotic.

And it was only the beginning.

CHAPTER 25

The darkness was broken up by thin strips of light, barely enough to illuminate. Just enough to tease. She was naked, coated in sweat, sliding against another body. Many bodies. Hands touched her, caressed her, coaxed a moan from her mouth. Two fingers found their way along her tongue. She sucked on them for a moment, caught up by the frenzy. Two more fingers slid in between her legs.

The lights flickered faster, a strobing effect. Her body found skin everywhere she moved, slick and ready. Sighs and grunts filled her ears. Fingers working away at her drew her closer to orgasm as she felt warmth pour over her. Liquid warmth. Coated in a stickiness now. A sea of bodies fucking in blood. Her blood.

More fingers gripped her hair in a fist as a nipple brushed against her mouth, the...

Audrey was ripped from the dream by the sound of the door being kicked in. Jarred awake, she almost fell off the bed as she tried to get her bearings. Two people were storming into their room, the man in front scowling at her.

"What the fuck!" exclaimed Elliot, leaping off his spot on the other bed.

The man backhanded him with the butt of a pistol, sending her brother crashing back into an end table. The woman frowned down at Elliot, and looked ready to help him up, but turned back to Audrey. While hers was pointed at the floor, the man's gun was pointed directly at Audrey's face.

"Are you Audrey Lynn Darrow?" he asked.

"Yes?"

"You're coming with us."

"Like hell I am!"

"You don't have a choice."

"Who the hell are you people?"

"We're the people who save the world from freaks like you most days."

"Cute."

"Today, however, we..."

A shout from outside pulled his attention away. If it was possible, he frowned even deeper.

"Watch them," he said to the woman.

Audrey glanced over at her, a young woman who didn't look much older than she. "Do you mind if I put on my shorts as opposed to sitting here in my underwear?"

The woman holding the gun sighed and nodded.

"Elliot, are you okay?" asked Audrey.

"Just pissed off," he said, getting up.

"Stay on the bed, please. I really don't want to have to shoot you."

Shots rang from outside, punctuating her statement.

"Jesus, what the hell are they shooting at?" asked Elliot.

"I don't know," said the woman, her face growing dark.

The woman moved to the door to peer out. Elliot looked over to Audrey and motioned for her to hurriedly get her shoes and shorts on, grab her purse. He put his own shoes on and snagged the keys to the car. Audrey was glad that they hadn't bothered dragging any luggage in for once. More gunshots and yells echoed from outside.

Elliot made to sneak up behind the woman and rush her, but just as he was ready to move, she bolted from her spot by the door. Scrambling to take her place, Audrey and Elliot looked out across the parking lot and witnessed a battle escalating. People, like the one who had attacked them at the casino, over a dozen of them. Mutilated faces and dressed in white rags. They attacked like pack animals, stalking the two who had broken into their room plus another man who lay wounded. It was taking a flurry of bullets to drop them, a single shot doing little to slow them down.

Elliot grabbed Audrey's hand and they raced to the car. She could hear the lead man bellowing after them, but he was far too busy with the horde of whatever those things were to come after them. The car peeled out of the parking lot, leaving her kidnappers to their fight in the glow of the taillights.

Beating on the steering wheel, Elliot finally began to lose his cool. "What the holy hell was all that?"

"Inanis said there were people after me who wanted me to use my powers. They think it's my duty to save the damn world."

"That guy didn't seem too happy about the idea."

"No, he didn't."

The man's words ran through Audrey's head. He'd called her a freak. She assumed it was because she was the Crimsonata. Just because she came from a magical bloodline, that didn't make her *that* different, did it? Maybe some people thought it did. Great, bigots on one side, monsters on the other. On top of that, she didn't like the idea that there was more than just the one of those creepy people in white.

"What do we do now, Audrey?"

Audrey didn't know. She didn't know how they had found them. Did they track Elliot's credit card somehow or have some crazy ninja skills? Maybe they had some witch in a cage somewhere looking at a map. She had no idea what they were dealing with. At least Audrey was relatively sure that these people didn't want to kill her. No, they just wanted to take choice away from her. Make her a slave.

She wasn't against discovering what her birthright was, what it meant to be the Crimsonata. But it would be by her choice, on her terms. No one would take that away from her, make her a puppet for their own mission. Honestly, a little more information is all she really wanted. The ability to make an informed decision.

Reaching over, she squeezed Elliot's hand. "Keep driving."

"To where?"

"I don't know, north."

She'd have him get a few hundred dollars in cash out of an ATM just to be safe and then they'd live off that for a while. For now she needed to think. They needed to be more proactive. She had an idea, but it wasn't a good one. She hoped she could think of a better one before the sun came up.

CHAPTER 26

Binici poured out some extra cat food and stared down at the bowl. She had no idea how long she would be gone. Hopefully not more than a few days. She'd only packed clothes for four days at the most. Everything was rapidly becoming more chaotic by the minute.

Going around the house, she checked all the windows to make sure they were closed and locked. There had never been any crime problems in her neighborhood, but she was a stickler about such things. Just as she was about unplugging her computer and a number of other appliances. It wasn't that she had real fears, but Binici spent a lot of time worrying about What-If's.

It was strange, because she generally wasn't an anxious woman. If anything, she just considered herself prepared. Contingency plans for contingency plans. Spontaneity was a dirty word, something reserved for children and imbeciles. Granted, it didn't leave her much of an entertaining life, but Binici was perfectly fine with that. It was also why she was quite displeased with the current state of affairs.

While affiliated with the Wall, she hadn't truly logged any field time and she preferred it that way. She was an academic, her area of expertise was research. The plan never necessarily involved her dealing with Audrey Darrow directly, although she did see the wisdom in it. Honestly, she just wished she would've had more time to prepare.

Faure really dropped the ball on this one. He threw this at her, with very little information, and now wasn't answering his phone.

Back at her desk, she was transferring most of her notes on the Crimsonata to her tablet. Granted, she had a majority of it memorized, but depending on the circumstances, Audrey might need to be reassured of her lineage. Of her importance. Binici could appreciate how overwhelming it might be to hear such grandiose tales.

Her phone rang, and she snatched it up immediately. "Faure?"

"What? No, but I'm looking for that shithole, too."

"Who's this?"

"My name is Hayden. I'm with the Wall. Faure gave me your number."

"Oh, of course. Did you get Audrey Darrow?"

"No, she got away. That was, as we were attacked by a gang of disfigured people that didn't want to die. Faces shorn of all features, finger bones sharpened to points, dressed in white rags."

"What?"

"Exactly. I've never seen anything like them. Weren't expecting them either. They severely injured one of my men and depleted my resources. Plus, like I said, we lost the Crimsonata. We had shit intel on this. Faure isn't answering, so I called you."

Binici was stunned. "Well, I've certainly never heard of anything like you're describing. Definitely not related to the Crimsonata lore, so it must be from external planes, sent here to kill her. You got caught in the crossfire, so to speak."

"So to speak?"

"Listen, I've only spoken to Timothy once since this began, and that was briefly last night. He's changed plans on both of us. He says the higher ups want me to approach Audrey and bring her in, in Ohio. I'm leaving for Cleveland here in twenty minutes."

Hayden sat quiet for a few moments. "The council approved the plan?"

"That's what I'm assuming. Timothy had everything set up at a location and..."

"I'll meet you in Cleveland," he said, then hung up.

Binici frowned at the phone and shook her head. She didn't even get a chance to tell him about the safe house in Eldridge, Ohio. It was no matter, all would be dealt with later.

She didn't even get to sleep, instead getting everything ready through the night. She could always catch a few winks on the plane, flying from California to Ohio. She didn't travel often, so she had sprung for a first-class ticket. A few vodkas and her earphones and she'd be snoozing.

It had been almost ten years since Audrey had actually met Emily Binici. Binici wondered if the young woman would even remember her. She had been such a quiet girl. Intelligent but distant. Binici kept track of her over the years, always looking for some sign of... well, the professor wasn't entirely sure what. That Audrey had discovered her path as the Crimsonata, yes, but how to determine the truth of that, Binici had no real idea. That the barriers were still breaking down only confirmed that Audrey had yet to flow.

Sometimes she teased herself, toyed with the idea of what life would've been like if she had adopted Audrey. She could've shown the girl her destiny and saved everyone this pain, saved the world this heartache. She'd never found anyone she gave a damn about enough to marry, and a kid had never been something she wanted, but maybe Audrey. She knew it was a fantasy, but it was something she thought about when she was feeling melancholy.

When forced to admit it, Audrey was the closest thing she had to family. She had been secretly watching the girl grow up since she was fifteen. She could've intervened, could've done more, but she hadn't. There was no reason Audrey should remember her, she hadn't made her presence known. Audrey was just more research.

Binici rolled her suitcase out to the car and put it in the trunk. Backing out of the garage, she went through the mental checklist of all the things that needed turned off, closed, unplugged, and removed. Feeling confident that the house would be safe while she was gone, she turned out of her driveway and down the road. Deciding to be positive about the whole trip, she powered up her stereo and put on The Beatles.

Singing along, she tried not to think about the next few days and what they would hold for Audrey.

CHAPTER 27

He could feel it, the will of the Ovessa all around him. Parking his car, Faure stepped out and looked around. It looked like any other small American town, sans people. It was completely deserted, or so it appeared to him. He saw a car driving in, but he hadn't really been paying attention either. Now that he was, the stillness struck him.

The Ovessa throbbed elsewhere in the town, close, beckoning to him. Faure began to walk, letting the sensation lead. He wasn't terribly worried, his Most Holy had chosen him.

Passing by a small sandwich shop, he noticed blood splattered on the inside of the window. He paused to glance inside and saw a body on the floor. A young woman lay crumpled in a heap, her throat slashed. The knife was still clutched in her hand. He thought he could see feet sticking out from behind the counter. With a shrug, he kept going.

Another block, and Faure began to rethink leaving his car behind. It seemed a good idea at the time. Everything was moment by moment now. Honestly, when he considered it, he was surprised he had the presence of mind to navigate the car this far. He was manic, reactionary, but it felt good.

He had travelled through half another block when the shot rang out. He didn't duck or run, but simply stood still. The bullet had struck the ground a few feet away from him. He craned his head around to peer at the small parking lot where it logically would have come from. After a minute of waiting, he held up his hands in a submissive gesture and began walking again. He made it about four steps before a trio of people rushed around the cars toward him.

Faure examined them with something close to pity. An elderly man in a frayed shirt and paint-spotted jeans, a teen boy in a basketball jersey, and a little girl no more than ten. The old man kept the gun trained on him as they crossed the street. All three looked exhausted.

"Who are you, what are you doing here?" asked the old man.

"My name is Timothy Faure, and I'm going for a walk."

"He's one of them, Tony," said the boy.

"One of what?" asked Faure.

"Don't you know what's going on here?" asked Tony, the old man.

"I just got to Eldridge," said Faure. "I was supposed to meet a friend for lunch. But he wasn't there and there's no one around. Hell, my cell's battery died, too."

"Phones won't work anyhow, not since they got here."

"What are you talking about?" Faure asked, playing it out.

"It's a long story."

"Well, will you stop pointing that at me? Especially with the trigger mechanism loose, that thing could go off at any time," said Faure.

Faure had no idea what he was talking about, making the nonsense up. But he had a suspicion that Tony didn't know anything about guns either, given the ridiculous cowboy stance he was using. Sure enough, he turned the gun in his hand to look at the trigger. Faure reached out and snatched the gun right out of the old man's hands.

"Wait..." Tony began.

"No," said Faure before shooting him in the face.

The old man fell dead to the sidewalk, the little girl ran off screaming back through the parking lot. The boy scrambled backwards, his eyes darting back and forth between Faure and Tony's body.

"Feel free to run. The Ovessa will claim you eventually."

The boy ran.

Tucking the gun in his waistband, Faure carried on down the road. Here and there he saw a curtain drawn back, or a shadow move, but he was left alone. Perhaps the remaining citizens of Eldridge saw what had transpired, most likely they just didn't care. The town was imploding, and they knew their demise was imminent. Those who had been unable to escape the pull of power had found a place to cower and hide out until the end, to wait until the lure of that power was too great and they gave in. Because all would eventually give in.

Finally, after walking a handful of blocks, he saw it. It had once been a magnificent motel, decades ago. Its decay only served to make it a more majestic seat for the Ovessa. Up the stone steps, he tried the great double doors, but found them locked. Walking around the side of the building, he found a service entrance. Whispers slid to him as the door opened. Pausing, he listened as the sounds ran over him, entrancing him.

He had made it to the first landing when he saw them, dozens of them. Marked in honor of the Ovessa, stripped down to the barest of flesh. Free from the identifying marks of humanity, cleansed of their personality, they wore the adornments of their class distinction. The Invocated. Faure was awed at the beauty they represented, the truth and purity.

The Invocated stared at him but made no aggressive moves. They parted as he passed, the razor-tip finger bones still at their sides. For a time he merely walked among them, soaking in their glory. Their skin had a mucous-like substance thinly coating most of its surface, parts of the flesh greying and mottled. *They had been reborn as a superior species,* thought Faure.

The room led to an antechamber, which in turn led to a massive lounge. Here, even more of the Invocated loitered about as did other creatures far beyond Faure's imagination. Monstrosities that looked like three legged hairless apes removed whimpering humans from shackles on the wall. Giant, slavering mouths drooled all over their charges as they were carried like infants across the room. Most had long ago lost their sanity and didn't even notice. They were slapped down onto a table of beating, living meat, six such tables lined up in a row and taking up most of the lounge floor. There, giant spider-things saw to the esoteric surgeries that created the new breed of earthlings. They sliced and pasted, grew and molded. A light opened above one nearly rebirthed member of the Invocated, and Faure rushed forward, only to be denied the radiance.

"A would-be mote in the Ovessa's light," came a voice.

Faure looked past the activity on the meat tables and saw two thrones, and the figures sitting in them. The memories came rushing back to him of that all too-brief time he had touched his Most Holy. He knew the Ovessa had its Voice here on earth, but he hadn't thought it was so literal. He hadn't expected avatars.

He stepped past the creatures who ignored him as easily as did the Invocated. Peering up at the two, he examined them, and they smiled down at him. Clad only in black robes, currently thrown back, they were composed of what appeared to be an amalgamation of bone, gristle, tooth, talon, tendon, and ligament. Red eyes burned in black sockets and liquid hair spilled over their shoulders, black as ink and always flowing.

"Everything is biomechanical," whispered Faure.

"Bleat louder, little meat."

"This is all bioengineered at the will of the Ovessa. I understand now. Oh, the Most Holy is indeed great!"

"Interesting. I am the Sigh, and this is the Spittle. The Ovessa sought to try contact through the barrier and it would seem to have worked."

Faure fell to his knees. "I beg you, let me bask in the Ovessa's light once more!"

"No," said the Spittle with a smile. "You do not deserve such an honor."

Faure scrambled toward them on his hands and knees. "But, but... oh, but I have tricked the Crimsonata into coming here so that you can kill her! She'll be here soon."

The Sigh glanced at her beloved. "That could be very beneficial. Besides, I see no reason to waste the first successful cross-barrier Sympathectomy."

"This human is unique," said the Spittle. "Let us make him so."

CHAPTER 28

They had been driving all night and were in Kentucky. Audrey wasn't entirely sure how they ended up going back west, but they had. It didn't matter. They had switched out who was driving at one point, the other sleeping. Now they were just heading north. For some reason, in her head, that just felt right. She had taken the last exit a hundred miles back that put them on this route and she hoped Elliot wouldn't be pissed.

She had spent a lot of time thinking. Thinking about her life up until now, the way things could have been different, and how things were going to have to play out from here. As crazy as her mother was, Audrey really wished she hadn't died. She had carried all that bitterness and resentment for a long time, but there it was. She had never really wanted her mom to die, she felt abandoned. She was even more conflicted now, knowing that her mom had driven her dad away because of her Crimsonata beliefs.

The thing was, that was then, and this was now. She was playing Murder by Death softly through the stereo while Elliot snoozed next her, driving aimlessly across America, on the run. This had to stop. It would be one thing if it was only her, but she couldn't do this to Elliot. She knew full well he'd stay with her no matter how bad it got.

She had an idea, although she had no idea if it would work. A rest stop was coming up on her right and she veered off towards it. Fortunately, there weren't many people here. A few trucks and a handful of cars. Pulling down to the end, she parked, hoping not to wake Elliot.

No such luck.

"Hey," he said groggily. "You need to switch?"

"No, just stay here."

"What?"

Audrey got out of the car and marched over toward a picnic table. It stood next to a large oak tree and gave her some amount of cover. She hoped it was enough. People would probably still notice, though.

"Inanis!" she called out. "Inanis, can you hear me? God damn it, I need to talk to you! Inanis! Inanis!"

She could feel the air splitting behind her and spun. He stood there in his suit and red rose, looking perturbed.

"Not really how this works, Audrey. I'm not your fucking guardian angel."

"You were the other night."

"I have my own stakes in this. So what do you want?"

"We were attacked. Well, it's complicated. We were attacked by those people who want to kidnap me as the Crimsonata and then those people were attacked by the creatures with the fucked-up faces."

"The Invocated," said Inanis.

"What?"

"The folks with the fucked-up faces? They're called the Invocated. The thrall of the Ovessa. Chances are you'll see more of them."

"Awesome. That's just what I wanted to hear. In any case, I wanted to ask you about being the Crimsonata. You seem to know shit."

"I'll answer what I can."

"Like... does it hurt? Do I have to cut myself open and bleed out?"

Inanis sighed. "You bleed to feed the Outer Gods, but you do not bleed your own blood. When the time comes to perform the ritual, your body produces a magically-rich ichor that seeps from your pores. It comes from inside you but does not beat through your heart. From what I understand, the sensation has been different for every Crimsonata."

"Don't bleed your own blood," mumbled Audrey, remembering her childhood fears.

"That 'blood' is drawn up into the celestial gates where it is supped upon by the primordial entities that engineered the multiverse. They don't need this to survive in any capacity, but only do it as a form of entertainment."

"My life is a hobby to them?"

"Not even your life, just what flows through it."

"Jesus! So if I do this, I have to commit to this for the rest of my life. And have a daughter that I damn to this life or we have the same problem all over again."

"As the Crimsonata, your body will reject any XY sperm. You'll only be able to have daughters. Just so you know."

"You're not helping matters here," said Audrey.

"But I will, just not now. You've got a telephone call coming. Get back to the car."

And with that, he vanished.

Swearing to herself, she raced back to the car just as the phone started ringing. She pulled it out of her purse, Elliot fumbling awake again in the passenger seat. She didn't recognize the number but figured since Inanis mentioned it, it must be important.

"Hello?"

"Hello, is this Audrey Darrow?"

"Yes, who's this?"

"Audrey, you probably don't remember me, but my name is Emily Binici."

Of all the random people. "Yes Professor, of course I remember you. You bought me a poster that day at the university. I still have it. I'm sorry, I'm not in California right now, but..."

"My dear, I need to talk to you about something called the Crimsonata."

Audrey went cold. "What do you know about it?"

"Audrey, I'm the world's foremost expert on Crimsonata lore."

Silence. Trying to wrap her mind around what Professor Binici had just said.

"Are you there?" asked Binici.

"I'm here."

"I'm guessing you know what the Crimsonata is then. And you probably know there are people after you. I'm just about to board a plane for Cleveland and I'll be staying at the Marriott. Please come find me, I'll answer any questions you have."

"How..." Audrey began. "How do I know..."

"This is not a trap, not some scam. If anything, this is the culmination of my life's work and something I should have done for you years ago. I was simply too scared to get out from behind my books."

"Maybe, and that's a strong maybe, we can be in Cleveland by tonight."

"I hope to see you again, Audrey. I really mean that."

She hung up and turned to her baffled brother. "I need to catch you up on the last fifteen minutes."

CHAPTER 29

The sunlight cut down from the sky, bright and harsh. It was far too hot to be standing outside in cargo pants and boots, but Roma knew better than to even think about changing. There was a fine line concerning what you wore on a mission, a line between blending in and staying geared up. She had a small caliber gun concealed under one pant leg, a knife under the other.

A young man in scrubs walked by and smiled at her, but she didn't notice in time to smile back. He probably thought she was just another concerned family member standing outside the emergency room entrances, waiting on news. Maybe someone who had been on a camping trip, based on her attire. Yes, Roma liked that bit of fantasy.

She took another sip of the apple juice she had gotten out of a vending machine and stared at the parked ambulances. They had brought Greer here in the back of the SUV, him spilling blood everywhere. Those things had almost completely taken off his left arm, nearly gutted him. He was stable now, the wounds in his stomach not as bad as they had looked, but the doctors weren't sure if they could save the arm.

The creatures had been horrific, their faces scraped clean of any fleshy features. With bulging eyes, they had come in waves, desperate to kill. She still wasn't sure if they had elongated nails or talons, or what was going on with their fingers. Even headshots hadn't necessarily dropped them, each of them needing a good four or five bullets each. It was a miracle that neither she nor Hayden had been injured. They had only survived because Hayden had herded them toward the SUV and their extra rounds.

But now their rounds were cut down by half and the team was a member down. Roma assumed they would be called off the mission and another cell would be activated. Not according to Hayden. Oh no, he had taken this personally, of course. Although she heard everything Binici had said to him, his phone's volume cranked up all the way, Hayden still blamed the Crimsonata for the attack. For one of his men getting hurt. For her escaping in the chaos, as if she planned it.

She had a number for the Council in case of emergencies. Roma sipped her apple juice and wondered if this counted. There was no way Hayden was going along with the script, especially if the mission was as important as they were led to believe. This whole operation, in its present state, could no longer be sanctioned. Going over a lead's head was considered a sort of career suicide, but this seemed like the kind of thing they would want to know about.

Slipping the phone out of her pocket, she pulled up the contacts screen. Peering at it, she willed herself to make the call. Her indecision was rendered moot, however, when Hayden came storming out of the hospital. Slipping the phone back into her pocket, she looked up to meet his gaze.

"Well?"

"He's probably going to lose the fucking arm," grumbled Hayden.

"Jesus, that's horrible."

"There's nothing more we can do for him here. We have a mission to accomplish."

Roma stared at the lid to her apple juice container. "Hayden, shouldn't we transfer this to another cell now that we're a man down?"

"Another cell would just have to be brought up to speed, and time is a factor. Binici says she's meeting the Crimsonata in Cleveland, so we go there. She'll lure it in and then we strike. It's simple."

"It?"

"What?"

"You just called Audrey Darrow an 'it.' She's a twenty-four-year-old woman."

Hayden scowled. "The Crimsonata isn't natural, it doesn't belong in this world of ours. You better get your head screwed on straight, Roma, and get in the game."

She took another sip of her apple juice as he stomped off across the parking lot. Now that she thought about it, even if she made that call, Hayden probably wouldn't back off. Whatever had brought him to the Promethean Wall had made him a zealot, filled him with a complete and total hatred of anything supernatural. Roma understood that the world didn't work like that. Yes, people needed to be protected from the things lurking in the shadows, but there were things out there that could just as easily be used as tools, too. Hayden called for genocide, Roma called for cohabitation with a healthy dose of suspicion.

Either way, once this mission was over, she was done with this cell. She couldn't work with Hayden anymore. She wanted to stay with the Wall, but she'd go to Alaska if she had to. Peru. Russia. Whatever.

Tipping back the bottle, she finished the last of the apple juice. The golden delicious highlight of her day. Now she had to ride in silence with Hayden for hours as they made their way north. Coming up on the SUV, she saw that he had already finished rearranging the bags after taking Greer's things into him. Roma stopped long enough to grab her satchel from the back and bring it into the front seat before climbing in.

Hayden fired up the engine and pulled out, Roma looking for her earbuds. The Glitch Mob came thumping out as she laid her head against the passenger side window and watched the hospital disappear. It would have been nice if she could have played the music through the car speakers, but Hayden didn't listen to anything when he drove.

She hoped she could contain the situation when they got to Cleveland, keep everything calm and professional. She was actually glad to have Binici's presence. Although Hayden didn't have much patience for academia, he might actually listen to an expert. All this Crimsonata lore. Honestly, Audrey Darrow had just seemed like a terrified young woman, totally normal. Roma had been wrong before, though.

Roma just wanted this mission done.

CHAPTER 30

Lutton, Pennsylvania wasn't like Southard or even like Eldridge. Oh, it was small, with only a population of slightly over three thousand, but it was a prosperous village. Its location was fortuitous, less than an hour's drive from a number of billion-dollar industries that had not suffered in the recession. The citizens of Lutton went to their jobs, day in and day out, returning to their beautiful little village, always content in the belief that the horrors of the world existed elsewhere.

Even Sheriff Gibbons believed that, and he saw the worst of what Lutton had to offer. Not that it was all that bad. Speeding tickets for the most part. Drunk and disorderly, the occasional bust for pot. Sure they had their occasional domestic dispute, or bout of robberies, maybe some delinquents causing mischief, but nothing he and his deputies couldn't handle. There hadn't been a murder in Lutton since the 1990's when Pauly Shannon had shot his old man while drunk, and the only instance of hard drugs had been a single meth bust two years ago. No, Lutton was a good, safe village.

That was why the screams bothered Sheriff Gibbons so much.

The sun had just begun to set when he heard them. He had stepped outside to have his one cigar of the day before his evening loop through town. His last loop before he called it a day and let the night shift take over. At first, he thought it was just kids playing, but more voices rang out. Strong, shrill, ongoing. Gibbons took another puff and listened. It seemed to be coming from the north end of town. Swearing, he stubbed out his cigar and climbed into his cruiser.

Taking the streets at a normal speed, he couldn't hear the screams anymore. He was going to be pissed if it was just kids screwing about. Turning onto Main Street, he passed the ice cream shop, the barber, the used books store, and a thrift store. There weren't many people out for this time on a summer evening.

More screams echoed out of the encroaching night. Gibbons slowed down and listened. He couldn't tell where they were coming from. He started to get out of his car when two teenagers came bolting across the street. One tumbled to the ground in front of him. At first Gibbons was pissed, thinking kids were indeed messing around, until he saw the blood. It was streaming down the arm of the boy whom had fallen.

"What the hell is going on?" asked Gibbons.

"Sheriff, they're everywhere!" exclaimed the bleeding teen, clutching his arm.

"Who?"

The other one pointed. "Them!"

Gibbons spun to see five people dressed in white come shambling out from between the buildings. Their faces were all cut up and they had some kind of slime all over their bodies. And with the last vestiges of daylight dying, it was like the village exploded into violence. Screams ripped through the air, echoing and piercing. People ran everywhere, fleeing the horrors in white who gave chase. In every case that Gibbons witnessed, in those few moments, the people of Lutton were always caught, dragged down hard to ground, and butchered. The nearest white-clad lunatics were already red of tooth and claw.

Gibbons pulled out his gun and fired. He hit three of them, but only felled one. They kept coming.

"Get in the fucking car!" he bellowed.

He jumped in and the two teens tried to do the same. The first made it in, but his friend, the one with the injured arm, was dragged back. Gibbons pulled away as the boy's ragged screams rang out behind him. Swearing, he tried to navigate through the melee, trying to make it back to the station. In the backseat, the one boy he saved sobbed. He couldn't have been older than fourteen.

Everywhere, they were everywhere. People were ripped through their living room windows, pulled out through their battered front doors. Slaughtered on their lawns, their entrails gored out and their faces shredded. The elderly were skinned alive, the newborn were pulled apart. The entire village of Lutton was being systematically murdered in the most atrocious ways possible.

Bashing his way through roads, gaping at the nightmare that had come to his town, Gibbons finally managed to get his car back to the station. He let the kid out of the back and raced inside. He needed back up, he needed more guns. It was shift change, so he should have the three deputies from afternoon and the three from night still inside, if they weren't already out dealing with the madness.

Gibbons ran inside, slipped, and fell. He slammed his head against a filing cabinet. Groaning, he slowly reached up to rub his head and stopped cold. His fingers were covered in blood. His whole back was soaked with blood.

"Oh hell," came a whisper from the kid behind him.

Slowly getting to his feet, Gibbons looked around. The room still smelled of gunpowder. Not that it had helped the four of his deputies that lay in pieces, scattered around the room. The nearest had bled out across the floor, where the sheriff had slipped.

"Guns, where are the guns?"

Making his way across the room to where all of their equipment was stored, he heard a noise behind him and assumed it was the kid. He punched in the code to the gun safe and opened it, appraising his options. He hoped it would be enough.

"Kid, you know how to shoot?"

Nothing.

Gibbons turned. The kid was gone. Fled, hiding, or dead, it didn't matter. There were easily a dozen of the things in white in the room, staring at him. They began to draw closer.

"Why?" asked Gibbons. "Why here, why us."

They didn't answer. He could see now in the station lights that their fingertips were bone, sharpened to points. They all looked nearly identical with their faces carved up like that. They smelled like a pile of rotting wet leaves.

"I won't make it fucking easy for you," growled Gibbons.

He tried to pull a gun off the shelf and load it, but the creatures were on him before he ever got the chance. They killed him just as they had killed everyone else in Lutton, no survivors this time. That tale was already told.

And there were more still to tell.

CHAPTER 31

During the entire drive to Cleveland, Audrey planned on what she was going to say to Binici. The answers she would demand from the woman, the truth. Audrey would see that everything played out in a manner that she set, no games, no skirting the issues. But now, standing in front of the hotel, so much of that evaporated, blown away in the wind that battered at them from the nearby airport.

She had fond memories of Binici, a woman who showed her kindness when Audrey had been flailing. It tore her open to think that this person was involved, or worse, had known this secret about her. Her paranoia flared, seeking routes of escape.

"We don't have to do this," said Elliot.

Grinding her teeth, Audrey replied. "Yes we do."

Binici had texted them and said to meet in the bar. They went inside and glanced around for a moment, getting their bearings. Elliot found a small display that showed them the way and they followed a long corridor past a conference hall full of people, likely some type of convention. The hall spilled out into a spacious, well-furnished room of red leather, fumed oak, and cream-colored walls. The bar lined one whole wall, staffed by three bartenders. There weren't many people inside, so it was easy to spot Binici standing there right away.

She hadn't aged all that much since Audrey had seen her last. A little greyer, a little heavier. Her eyes shown as Audrey walked up to her and for a moment Audrey thought the woman was going to hug her. Instead, she just smiled and gestured to the seats in the booth next to her.

Hand raised to get the waiter's attention, she asked, "What would you like? I'm buying?"

"I'm fine, thanks," said Audrey, glaring at the woman.

"Screw that, I'll get a Long Island. Thank you," said Elliot.

The waiter scurried over and Binici said, "You better make it three Long Island's, just in case."

Audrey screwed up her face but didn't know what to say. She hadn't expected this. She had to reestablish control.

"What do you know about the Crimsonata?"

"Quite a bit. I've been studying the phenomenon in one form of another for almost thirty years. I'm tempted to say I'm the leading living expert, next the Crimsonata herself."

"Why study the Crimsonata?" asked Elliot.

"At first, it was purely academic. Correlating data across historical records for studies on the Sacred Feminine. I was shocked to discover this tiny bit of overlap, this blood ritual and linked mythology, something never before explored. Not only was this my ticket into the textbooks, I was hooked. But the more I learned, the more I was pulled into something I didn't fully understand."

"Because the Crimsonata was real," said Audrey.

"Yes," said Binici. "Along with so many other things I didn't think existed."

Audrey shook her head. "Did you know when you met me?"

Binici gave her a sad smile. "My dear, I knew what you were when I met you. I had an inkling when I met your mother."

The revelation shot through Audrey and silenced her next comeback. The waiter brought their drinks, and Audrey chugged down half of hers in one go. At least the professor had the decency to look embarrassed by her confession. But more was to come.

"Once I knew the Crimsonata was real, and knew it was you for sure, I watched you. Checked up on you. Nothing invasive, just drove by your place every now and again. Browsed your social media. I wanted to do more, but I didn't know what to do. I should've been there for you earlier, but I'd already failed you in that."

"And do what for me?"

"Just... been your friend."

Audrey would've been angrier at the invasion if the old woman didn't look ready to cry. She didn't know if she was a research project or a lost kitten to Binici. Either way, it made her uncomfortable. Either way, it was just another person who didn't really know, but expected her to be a certain way. She was getting tired of that.

"So what now?" asked Elliot. "What made you track Audrey down now?"

"A Crimsonata has always flowed, for countless centuries. Sometimes only one, often many. While you are one, you haven't accessed your powers. A Crimsonata hasn't flowed since your mother died almost twenty years ago. There are repercussions to that."

"Yeah, we've heard this story," mumbled Audrey.

"Have you heard these stories?" asked Binici, sliding a small tablet out of her purse. She keyed up two news stories and handed it over to Audrey.

Audrey read the news articles with growing horror. Widespread death and injuries in the towns of Southard and Lutton. Thousands dead in both towns, all of Lutton wiped out. The survivors of Southard all said the same thing about the assailants – disfigured people dressed in white.

"This is only the beginning," said Binici as Audrey's shaking hand passed the tablet to Elliot.

The waiter came back, and the professor kindly ordered them all more of the same. Audrey couldn't get the pictures out of her head. A shot of Lutton showed a street lined with body bags, the whole street, a mile long. That many dead in a night. Could she really stop this? Was she being selfish, childish, by still refusing out of principle? Even if she wanted to access her powers, right here in the hotel bar, she had no idea how to.

"I need to apologize about something else," said Binici. "The people after you, trying to kidnap you. I never thought it would come to that."

"You're connected to them?"

"Indirectly, yes. They're called the Promethean Wall. They're a global organization with ties to law enforcement, governments, corporations, universities, you name it. They're charged with protecting humanity from supernatural interference. Right now, you're considered our best defense against the abominations climbing up from the gutter realms, so they want to utilize you."

"Whether I like it or not."

"Sadly, yes."

"The gutter realms?" asked Elliot.

"The blood must flow to appease the gods. Without this, the barriers break down. The first barriers are the lowest, those holding back the gutter realms. Something in particular from one of these realms has taken a hold here on earth, one that wants dominion here, in the time before The Outer Gods break through and obliterate this universe."

Audrey polished off her second Long Island. "And I, using magical blood, will stop all of this?"

"Yes."

"I call such bullshit, but okay. Even if I wanted to, I have no idea how to. That's problematic to say the least. Shouldn't I have figured that out by now if I'm this chosen one?"

"That occurred to me as well. But listen, the Wall has a safe house here in Ohio. Audrey, please let me take you there. Elliot can come, too. We'll work on this together, figure it out. Let me help you save the world."

Audrey stared at the old woman, letting the words sink in. Maybe it was time to make a choice. Elliot, wide eyed, looked back and forth between her and Binici. She didn't trust the professor all that much, but that didn't really matter anymore.

People were dying out there. Maybe she could finally do something that mattered.

"Fuck it," said Audrey. "Let's save the world."

CHAPTER 32

It was the absolute appropriation of his entire body, his flesh given over to a higher calling. His mind laid bare and his will surrendered. Faure understood what was happening and he welcomed it, embraced it. This would make him a better servant for his Most Holy.

Lingering memories nagged at the back of his head. Reading in his backyard as a child, under the giant pine tree. Going fishing with his father that last time at the beach before they moved away from the coast. His fumbling with Susanna Rowling in her dorm room his sophomore year. Proposing to his wife outside that Italian restaurant in the rain, so unlike the scene he had planned. Working on his doctoral dissertation late into the night, fueled only by coffee and work ethic. All the things that had made up Timothy Faure, had comprised his life, were still there, but muted. Sealed away in a box, in an unused portion of his skull, ready to be discarded. Deleted.

A new meat table had been constructed for his procedure, one that pulsed with life. He had stripped down and was placed upon it, docile and compliant. He eagerly anticipated his transformation, his new life. Pain would be pleasure, the pleasure a blessing.

The Spittle and the Sigh walked around the table, watching as his body was washed down with caustic chemicals that stripped him of all his hair. Faure never let out a sound, reveling in the agony of his scorched skin.

"While the Crimsonata may indeed be coming, it is not swift enough to please the Ovessa," said the Spittle. "Other measures should be seen to."

The bone face of the Sigh pulled into a smile. "Perhaps it's time for something more direct."

Faure may have heard them speaking, but he was no longer able to fully comprehend their words. Needle-like appendages from creatures resembling giant centipedes had been injected down every limb and across his torso. Five of these insects quivered above him, their juices pumping into his body. It felt like poison, it felt like lava, and Faure clenched his jaw against it. He began to say a mantra in his head over and over, *For the Ovessa, For the Ovessa, For the Ovessa*. The pain did not cease.

Bones broke and re-healed. Muscles shifted and grew. Faure was enlarging. His skin tore wide open and was stitched back together when the spiders coated it with a foul-smelling powder. His pinky and ring fingers snapped and fell off to make room for the massive growth of his index and middle finger. His toes all but shriveled up into something resembling the front of a hoof. Between his legs, his cock split and blossomed into some new set of sexual organs, never before seen on earth.

"Do you think the barrier has thinned enough to send anything more than the Invocated?" asked the Spittle.

"If we can summon creations to us, we can send them to the Crimsonata," said the Sigh. "It's not a matter of power."

A single hole appeared above Faure, allowing just a small stream of light to shine down upon him. All of the suffering would now be worth it. Once more he would touch the majesty of the Ovessa. The beam of light began at his mutated genitals and worked its way up his body, searing a line into his still morphing flesh with its divine might. Although he had pledged to stay silent, he couldn't help but let out a whimper. The ray traveled up to his face and filled him, all of him.

All that had been Timothy Faure was burnt away in a cold, bright flash.

The circumference of the beam expanded, engulfing all of Faure's head. It began to rework the flesh like putty, melting down the bone into liquid. The entire head became something less than material, something almost non-corporeal. It flopped and shuddered and splashed in a confined space, each atom in continuous entropy. The entire head now a ravenous maw of cosmic chaos, always devouring.

"This new creation isn't ready yet," said the Spittle. "Have you something else in mind?"

"I thought the Bitter Born would wreak havoc nicely."

The Spittle gave the idea some thought. "Your experiment with the children acquired from here? At least then they might have a purpose other than shrieking. Unable to be repurposed as Invocated, they should have simply been culled."

"You lack imagination, my beloved. The Bitter Born, while unruly, will terrify the Crimsonata merely by their existence. And they are so vicious, so wild, they could easily destroy our jailer where the Invocated could not."

"As always, I defer to your wisdom," said the Spittle, giving her a short bow.

The Sigh looked over at what used to be Faure, his hairless pink body steaming. Its form was easily seven feet tall now, a mass of muscles, not all of them natural to human physiology. Two meaty fingers and a thumb twitched on each hand. The light had branded a single, scored mark up the center of the body, a row of six tiny nipples running up each side of the torso. The new head glitched and cascaded.

"In what will we adorn our latest kin?" asked the Sigh.

"What will we call it?" countered the Spittle.

"Another excellent question. But both will have to wait. Let me attend to the Bitter Born, rally them for the excursion."

The Spittle nodded and went to see to the preparations as the Sigh headed to the basement. All the while, the aberration that used to be Timothy Faure lay there, its mind blank and malleable. It recalled nothing of a wife, of academia, of a home. Nothing of the life it once had.

All it knew was hunger.

CHAPTER 33

Binici had offered to pay for their room, but Elliot declined. He had money, he could take care of them. He *wanted* to take care of them, but Audrey didn't seem to want to listen. Instead, she was striding down the hall on her short little legs, pointedly ignoring him.

"Will you just stop for a second?" exclaimed Elliot, grabbing at her arm.

She pulled away from his grip, angry. "What, Why?"

"Can we please talk about this?"

She folded her arms tightly and stared down the corridor, refusing to make eye contact. Elliot sighed. He just needed to catch his balance, get some dialogue going. Everything was happening so fast and he was being swept along. Usually he would be okay with that, but this time it was a bit more serious. This time, Audrey's life was at stake.

"How can you trust her after everything she told you?" Elliot asked. "You know this could be a trap."

"It very well could be, but I'd rather walk into it eyes open than be snatched out of my bed again."

"So that's it. You're giving up, you're giving in?"

"It's *my* life, *my* choice!" said Audrey. "I'm choosing to put an end to this nightmare. I'm making an informed decision. About as informed as I'm going to get."

Elliot didn't know what to say to that. She was right, of course. That didn't mean he liked it. He wanted to run, let the world burn. What did that say about him? Did that make him a good brother or a coward? He didn't really want to examine those thoughts too deeply.

Some random businessman strolled past them and nodded in Elliot's general direction as a greeting. The poor bastard's biggest concern was probably making it on time to his morning meeting. Meanwhile, the universe was being invaded by monsters. The absurdity of it made Elliot laugh. Audrey shot him a look.

"No, I'm not..."

His sentence was cut off by a disturbance at the end of the hall. The light flickered and bent, collapsing to a single point in the center of the corridor. A stench like chemicals and exotic incense filled the narrow passageway. Elliot began to back up, pulling Audrey with him. The anomaly split open like a wound in reality, and small creatures spilled out, flying through the air.

At first, he could only gawk at them. They were babies, human babies once. But now, they had wings grown from their backs, appendages that were similar in structure to those of a bat's. Skin so thin, you could see the blue veins running and pumping visibly beneath. The flesh of their bodies was just as delicate, almost transparent. The one nearest to them began to screech, its jaw unhinged from its skull like a snake's. As if it were clarion call, the others took to the sky and threw themselves at Elliot and Audrey.

They fled, around the corner and back down the stairs. They weren't far from the bar, from the exits. Feet pounded against the carpeted floor as the creatures beat pink wings behind them, gaining speed. The confined space was the only thing keeping them from catching up, the winged beast babies tumbling over each over in their flight. Down a short series of steps, they rounded the corner into a junction that could take them either to the bar or back down a hallway to the lobby. Elliot pulled one way, Audrey the other.

"What are you doing?" screamed Audrey.

"There are exits through the bar!"

Not wanting to let her argue any longer, Elliot pointed at the approaching flock and hauled Audrey into the bar. It had grown more populated in just the five minutes since they had left, people milling around. Binici stood by the bar with some other people and Elliot headed toward her.

It wasn't until he was almost upon her that he realized that the people she was talking to were the ones who had broken into their motel room the other night.

Elliot ran right up to the man, looked him in the eyes, and said, "I hope you have your guns."

"What?" asked the man, taking a step back.

That was when the flying creatures burst into the bar. There were six of them, flapping about in the high-ceilinged room, swooping in to attack when they saw an opening. Biting and gorging with those impossibly tiny mouths. The patrons ran screaming, some tried to hide under tables. A creature landed in a woman's hair and rode her to the ground, chewing off her face.

The bartender grabbed a fire extinguisher and was trying to spray one to little effect. He dropped the canister and ran behind the bar. Elliot picked up the spent device and wielded it like a club. The man from the Wall fired off two shots, missing, but hit one with a third. It went down, and he fired two more rounds into it to make sure. The woman dove under a table, dragging Audrey and Binici with her. When a creature followed, she shot it point blank in the face. A second shot to prove her point. She rolled back out from beneath the table and moved back toward her partner. Another creature came hurtling toward Elliot, and gripping the end of the fire extinguisher, he batted it against the wall. When it bounced to the floor, he ran over and bashed its skull into pulp with the spent fire extinguisher.

"Only two more," said the man from the Wall.

Right on cue, six more of the flying babies came shrieking their way into the bar.

"You had to," grumbled Elliot.

Everyone readied their respective weapons when the air waivered and folded next to Elliot. He jumped back as Mr. Inanis stepped through in his black suit and red rose on the lapel.

"Alright, enough of this," he said, making a hard gesture with his right hand.

Every single one of the creatures, dead or alive, burst into flame.

CHAPTER 34

For a moment, everyone was silent, everyone was still. That didn't last long. Sobs began to echo around the bar from the regular people caught up in the madness, the innocent by-standers. Audrey had seen at least two people killed by those things and knew there had to be more. Things that had been most likely been sent after her.

"Are you okay?' asked Binici, her eyes wide.

Audrey patted her hand and began to crawl out from beneath the table. She was halfway out when she was hauled to her feet by the man who had called her a freak at the motel. He held her at gunpoint again.

"What the hell, man?" said Elliot. "We came to you!"

"Hayden, let her go," said the woman.

Hayden didn't respond, nor did her let her go. His eyes burned into Audrey, full of hate. She could clearly see that, clearly see that he wanted to kill her as much as he had wanted to kill those flying abominations. To him, she and they were the same.

Inanis stepped over. "You just watched me telepathically burn eight creatures on a whim. Do you really want to do this?"

Hayden turned to him. "Witch," he said, the word spat out.

"A concerned citizen," replied Inanis.

"This isn't Audrey's fault. These denizens are after her because she's the only one who can stop them," said Binici, crawling out from under the table. "She must flow to save the world, quite probably the universe!"

"In return for a lifetime of servitude," yelled Elliot.

Hayden let go of her, but his eyes still drilled into her. "If it is your duty, then you will endure."

"All of you can seriously go fuck yourselves!" screamed Audrey. "It's my life, and I'll do whatever I want for whatever reasons. I'm sick of people dying, my heart can't take that. I'm *choosing* to be the Crimsonata because it will save lives."

Everyone stood there, listening to people rush out of the bar, the sobs of the people still in shock, and the sound of the oncoming authorities. No one really paid attention to the six people standing in a circle near the bar, deep in discussion. No one cared.

"What if there was a third option?" asked Inanis.

"What?" asked Audrey.

"What if you could free yourself from being the Crimsonata and still keep the barrier up at the same time?"

"Foul witch riddles," growled Hayden.

"You really are one-dimensional, you know that, right?" Inanis threw back at him.

"What are you saying?" asked Binici. "Some cosmic loophole?"

"That's exactly it. Go to the town as your former associate instructed. It's not exactly a safe zone though, I should warn you."

Binici squinted at him. "You know Timothy Faure?"

"I know everyone, Emily."

Binici backed up and ran into the bar, the color draining from her face.

"All five of you need to go, incidentally. Consider this the climax of a very long, very weird story. You don't have to, of course, but I'd recommend it."

"Why?" asked the woman from the Wall.

Inanis sighed. "Audrey Darrow, you will finally find purpose in your life. Elliot Byrnes, you will be the protector that your sister never had. Alec Hayden, you face the greatest supernatural threat to ever walk this earth in your lifetime. Allison Roma, you get to see a truth that most can't even conceive of. And Emily Binici, you finally, after all these years of study and research, will get to see the Crimsonata flow."

They all stood there, gaping at him. His words had cut deep, exposing exactly what all of them needed. It was too apparent, too real. Each of them knew they would go.

"Oh look, the police. Time for me to go. See you in Eldridge."

And he disappeared.

"You know, you said 'witch,' but," said Roma. "I've never met a witch remotely like that."

* * *

They were blaming it on bats.

It was a ridiculous story, but no one wanted to think about the alternative. Mutated babies with wings crafted from a lower dimension just wouldn't play on the nightly news. Seven people were dead, five injured. Everyone but those in their little party was in shock, and that wasn't to say they weren't also reeling.

Hayden still wanted to take Audrey in by force, but Roma stood firm against him. She pointed out that it probably wasn't smart to piss off a High Mage. There had been friction between the two ever since Inanis left. She was no longer taking his lead, no longer deferring to him. Something had broken between them and Roma didn't seem to show any inclination of repairing it. They had worked well enough together to smooth things over with the police concerning their discharge of weapons in the bar, something about concealed carry permits and special authorization. Audrey didn't understand all of it, but she assumed it had to do with the Wall. At one point, the detective to whom they had been talking had received a call, gone pale, and then promptly told them to have a nice night.

Binici tried to contact Faure again to no avail. Inanis's words about Eldridge lingered and the old woman was worried about what had happened to her friend. Audrey wanted to trust the professor, but just couldn't quite bring herself to do so. In many ways, that made her sad.

They sat at the bar talking to the cops for hours. The people from the hotel were beside themselves. Not only was the bar trashed, but customers were leaving in droves. A bat attack in Cleveland? Everyone knew it was cover up and that made them more terrified. The piles of ash that were once flying babies were being swept up as just another part of the mess.

Elliot stayed beside her the whole time, and while Audrey appreciated his dedication, she was beginning to feel like he didn't believe she could do this on her own. Yes, she knew she was an anxious, paranoid mess, but she had survived all these years just fine without him. He was overcompensating, and she knew that, but it was starting to become suffocating.

A bartender appeared behind the bar, offering free drinks to the victims. Audrey, Elliot, Binici, and Roma all lined up, Hayden standing there glowering at them. To make things easy, they all ordered double vodkas on the rocks, clinked glasses, and began drinking. Audrey peered at Roma, trying again to guess her age. Probably around twenty-six or twenty-eight. She decided Hayden didn't have an age, as he probably wasn't human.

Binici turned in her seat. "Can I ask you a question?"

"Sure."

"How long have you known that... individual who destroyed all those monsters?"

"Mr. Inanis? A few days. He just kind of appeared."

Binici nodded, eyes cast down. "He scares me."

"Scares me, too," said Roma. "That's some high-grade voodoo, Nth level. No incantations, no talisman. Well, maybe that rose. That's strange. Still, he's the most powerful spell caster I've ever seen."

"They all die the same," said Hayden.

"I have a feeling that this one doesn't," Binici said into her drink.

Audrey thought Hayden hadn't heard, but she saw him frown. Good. He needed his black and white world shaken. His belief in a bullet was sickeningly alpha male in her opinion, too.

She didn't know how Inanis's third option would pan out, didn't want to get too excited by it. She had been disappointed too many times. Eldridge, Ohio seemed like a weird place to go for all this, but one spot was as good as another. She had resigned herself to embracing her Crimsonata heritage but trying something else first was worth a shot.

Roma downed the rest of her drink just as the police cleared them to go. She stood up and stretched, looking at the rest of them. "We should all get a few hours of sleep then leave late morning, agreed?"

Hayden started to say something but was interrupted by Elliot. "I think that's a fantastic idea. I was already looking up Eldridge on the internet. It's only about two hours away."

Audrey downed the rest of her vodka. She stood up and adjusted her shorts. Part of her felt like she should be wearing something other than a tank top and cut offs when she faced this monumental event tomorrow, but that's all she had with her.

"If you try to run..." growled Hayden.

"Oh, give it a rest," snapped Audrey. "This isn't fucking about you."

With that, she turned away from him and left all of them standing by the bar.

CHAPTER 35

That night, while the Bitter Born were attacking a Cleveland hotel, the Invocated were invading another small town.

Jessica Fulmer hadn't been to sleep yet. She had been lying in bed, texting her boyfriend for hours. At sixteen, almost seventeen, she and Connor had been together all of their sophomore year. He wasn't perfect, but she loved him. She also wanted to start having sex with him, something he was strangely hesitant to do. Jess tried not to take it personally, tried to listen to his concerns about pregnancy, but it still stung. Most of their conversation that night had surrounded the topic.

There wasn't much for young people to do in Bolton, Pennsylvania besides get drunk and screw. The nearest movie theater was thirty miles away, the nearest mall another twenty miles past that. There were no coffee shops or skate parks, no teen clubs or youth organizations. They were simply expected to stay put, entertain themselves, and behave. As if that had ever worked in the history of humanity.

Most of Jess's friends were no longer virgins. She didn't consider it a big deal, just another hurdle to jump in life, something to get out of the way. It wasn't something precious like the bible-thumpers wanted you to believe, just another natural act. But it nagged at Jess that Connor didn't want to. Like she wasn't worth it. While she knew she wasn't a Hollywood model, she felt like she was pretty enough. And he swore up and down his undying devotion to her. She just didn't get it.

According to Connor, he had a deep-seeded fear of getting her pregnant, of ruining their lives. She tried to explain to him about this new-fangled invention called condoms, but he didn't seem convinced that these could save them from the curse of procreation. The conversation had gone like this, in circles, for hours, and Jess was beginning to reassess her relationship, based more on her boyfriend's revealed stubbornness than anything else. She'd never seen this side of him, it bordered on unstable.

It had become quite late and she'd had enough for one night. Saying goodnight, she thumbed out of the messenger app and climbed out of bed. The willowy redhead was supposed to go on a two-mile run in the morning with her best friend Gillian, but she had a feeling that she was going to skip out. She went downstairs to get some orange juice, skipping the glass and drinking right out of the carton.

That's when she heard the gurgling in the living room.

Setting the carton back in the fridge, she stepped into the living room. She hadn't recognized the noise, assumed the cat had gotten into something. It hadn't. It took her a few moments to understand the scene before her eyes. Her father on his knees, two people in white beside him, blood everywhere. Her father screaming at her to run.

Jess ran. Jess could run well, she was a premier track star. She bolted out of the house and across the lawn. Down the street and across to Mrs. Bailey's house. Banging on the door, words trying to form in her head, she didn't see the white form loom behind the window until it yanked open the handle. Jess screamed and kept running.

She saw them now, everywhere. She heard the screams. People dressed in white were murdering the town. People dressed in white with horrible faces were killing everyone she knew.

Gillian's house. She knew her best friend's dad was a gun nut. Jess crept inside, hoping they were safe. Gillian's mother,

Faith, was splayed out in the kitchen, entrails splattered across the floor. Her eyes stared vacantly at the ceiling. Jess choked back a sob. The woman had been like a mom to her since her own mother had died of cancer five years back. Creeping deeper into the house, she saw a pair of Gillian's old running shoes sitting by the basement door. Still hampered by bare feet, Jess slipped them on. She quietly called out her best friend's name but got no answer.

Further into the house, upstairs. The bedrooms, the bathroom, nothing. They weren't here. Jess hoped they had escaped. Now it was her turn. She made her way back down to the first floor and peered out of the windows. Nothing but darkness out there, silent and still. Jess considered waiting it out in here but couldn't bear to be near Faith's body. The pain was too personal, too acute.

She found a cell phone and assumed it to be Faith's, but it was password locked. Nobody had house phones anymore. She had left hers back at her own home.

She could run. She could sprint for miles, if need be. She was only dressed in shorts and a sports bra, but it was a warm evening. The highway wasn't far, and she could flag down a passing car. Get help. She could do this.

Jess eased the door open and stood in the shadows, psyching herself up. She couldn't think about Faith lying there dead, or about Gillian, or about Connor. She just had to run. Just run. She shot out from the door and took off through the neighborhood, rocketing past houses. She heard noises but ignored them. Forward, faster.

There were people lying on their lawns, gutted and draining. People torn through their windows. Children with their faces clawed off. Wetness everywhere, a sheen of blood that looked black in the night.

Jess ran, the people in white appearing, seeing her, following her. Jess ran, fleeing the horror, willing it untrue as she passed it. They came in at her from the sides, and she began to cry, tears filling her eyes. Foot after foot, just make it to the highway. The highway would save her.

The pain came out of nowhere and sent her to the ground.

She tumbled, rolling a few feet from the momentum. Dazed, she didn't have time to get back up before they surrounded her. Five, six of them. They backed off as a single one stood over her, straddling her. It stared down at her with too-large eyes, teeth revealed from lips cut away into a rictus. Sharpened fingertips reached down to her face.

Jess began to sob, the only sound in the street, until she began to scream.

CHAPTER 36

It had taken some rearranging, but Binici rode with Audrey and Elliot while the two from the Wall followed in their SUV. It had been a rough morning, no one yet trusting each other, but at least everyone was underway. Audrey was feeling the day a little harder than the others, for multiple reasons, and sucking down her second coffee while chain-smoking out the passenger window.

She didn't really care about the two from the Promethean Wall at this point. Roma seemed decent enough and she felt like Hayden had been put in his place by Inanis. If anything, she was sort of glad for the backup. They had experience in dealing with this kind of madness.

She still had no idea what Inanis was up to, but her wellbeing appeared tied to his own ends. She would roll with it for now. Roma thought he was some type of Super Sorcerer and Binici was terrified of him. Audrey just thought he was a bit of a prick.

No, today's issue was the lingering effect of another dream. The first dream she'd had was obviously something her pursuers had sent at her, but the second one had been something different. This was like the latter. It got inside her, touched her. She thought it had something to do with being the Crimsonata.

Even now, she could recall it.

There is a giant obsidian orb sitting in a desert. But it is not obsidian, it is not solid. It glistens and flows, liquid held in stasis. And it has the faintest red cast behind the black. A darkest crimson. Beneath this massive, surreal monument congregates thousands of women. They are of all nationalities

*and ages, all naked, and all rapt with religious fervor. They
wait, they're ready. The orb releases a tidal wave of itself in
all directions, although never running out, never ceasing to
be. The women are awash in a blood not theirs. I see through
all of their eyes.*

The entire experience was surreal, something hard to
recall, let alone put into words. It was more of a sensation and
an overpowering one at that. It left Audrey battling conflicting
feelings.

"You okay?" asked Elliot

"I'm fine."

"We don't have to..."

"Yes, Elliot, we do."

She didn't want to be short with her brother, but she'd had
just about enough of him, too. He'd become a little too
overprotective for her taste. This was her choice and she was
making it. They had gotten into a brief argument back at the
hotel, Elliot still wanting to run. He thought that because he
still had money that he could take care of her. He wasn't seeing
the bigger picture. Audrey had tried to spell things out for him,
but he was just too scared. She got that, she was too.
Eventually, she had to yell at him, and told Elliot to either get
on board or go home.

This was the first they had spoken since the blow up. They
had been listening to Explosions in the Sky quietly for the last
half hour. Binici used this opportunity to speak up.

"I feel like I need to apologize to you, Audrey."

"For what?"

"For not doing more. Doing more for you."

"Jesus, I didn't turn out that bad."

"No, no," said Binici. "I don't mean it like that."

Audrey twisted around in her seat so that she could look at
both Binici and her brother. "Listen, both of you. I know I'm
fucked up. I'm moody and twitchy and weird. I should probably
be on a handful of meds daily. But I've made it this far on my

own and I'll continue to do so. I'm a big girl, an adult. I can make choices for myself, and I don't need either of you taking care of me or feeling sorry for me. Are we clear on that?"

Elliot mumbled out a, "Yeah, sorry."

Binici smiled. "I never meant to imply that I was anything other than proud of you."

"What she said," added Elliot.

"I can do this, because I have to. Because there's been a lot of shit I haven't necessarily wanted to do that I've done. This time, however, it's more than that. It's the right thing to do. I need to stop people from getting hurt. That I can get behind. Maybe I've analyzed too many comic book movies, I don't know."

"I think your reasons for choosing to do this are exactly the right reasons," said Binici. "If anything, they make you a far better Crimsonata than your predecessors who only did it out of a sense of familial duty."

"And if Inanis is telling the truth, you won't have to do it long," said Elliot.

"I'm not even thinking about that right now," said Audrey.

Honestly, she wasn't. She was more concerned with stopping the things that were killing entire towns full of people. If she had the power to do that, she would, no matter what the cost. Part of her wanted to be the heroine of this story and save the day, a role she had only read about, watched on the screen. She knew she was damaged, not exactly a paragon of strength, but she would try.

Audrey knew she wasn't a good person, but she could do good. That's the best that most could hope for in life. To be better, to do better. And she was doing it for herself.

Growing melancholy, she began flipping through songs until she found something more upbeat. Landing on Panic! At the Disco, she took another sip of her coffee and tapped her fingers along with the beat. For her, it seemed appropriate music to go into battle.

CHAPTER 37

As per usual, Roma and Hayden drove in silence.

Hayden was more tense than usual, gripping the steering wheel so hard he was white-knuckled. Roma tried her best to ignore it, to chalk it up to him mentally preparing for Eldridge, but she knew better. Mostly the sneer on his face the whole time gave it away.

As soon as they entered the Eldridge area, something began to feel wrong to her. It was all too quiet. There should be more cars, more activity. The day was overcast, but it was more than that. The light looked wrong, somehow too dim. Everything had a greyish cast that shouldn't be there on a June afternoon.

She mentioned it to Hayden, but he only grunted. He had barely looked at her all morning. The rift between them was impassible now. Roma would have to put in for a transfer whether she wanted to or not. There was a good chance Hayden would put one in for her. That was fine, she was almost done here.

Still...

"Something is wrong with this whole town, Hayden. It's pretty apparent. There's no one anywhere."

No response.

"I hope that mage knows what he's talking about."

"He's a filthy mage and needs to be put down."

Roma gave him a sidelong glance. "You do realize there are adept cells in the Wall that use magic, right?"

His sneer deepened. "A fucking perversion of our calling. They are just as bad as the things we hunt."

Roma shook her head at him. She couldn't believe she never realized what a zealot he was. The adepts were sanctioned by the Wall to use magic in the fight against their supernatural adversaries. It was well-known, and for the most part, well-accepted. A fight fire with fire kind of attitude. That he felt so strongly against it said a lot.

"So all magic, anything supernatural, must be stamped out?" asked Roma.

"Yes Roma, it's not that hard."

"Good luck with that. I'm not sure your guns are going to do much against Outer Gods."

He didn't have much to say to that.

Hayden continued following the car with everyone else in it and Roma once again found herself thinking about the Crimsonata. Audrey Darrow was not what she had expected. She was so utterly normal. A short, relatively attractive blonde girl, a few years younger than her. Kind of skittish, somewhat weird, overall average. Roma had expected some kind of Amazonian goddess. That first time in the motel, she was convinced they had the wrong person. The girl had looked so terrified. Not what you pictured in a metaphysical super being.

She was glad Audrey had agreed to go along with the plan. She didn't want to have to force her, that just felt wrong. Plus, Hayden would have just made the whole thing a violent debacle. Also, it really was the right thing to do, saving the universe and all. But now with this third option proposed by the guy in the suit, Roma wondered how things were going to play out.

"You think the mage really has a viable plan?" asked Roma.

"I don't care."

"Well, you need to have an opinion, Hayden."

"It either works or it doesn't. Either way, the Crimsonata flows."

"Fair enough. And then this is over."

"If the plan doesn't work, we take the Crimsonata into custody. We hold her until she can procreate and continue on the bloodline. If it does work, then I can kill it before it ever becomes a threat again."

Roma gaped at him. "Are you listening to yourself?"

"What must be done."

"Those are *not* your orders, I guarantee that."

"Orders are irrelevant. This is bigger than the Wall and their short-sightedness."

Roma leaned back in her seat and came to a cold revelation.

She was going to have to kill Alec Hayden.

* * *

High above, the Ovessa bucked and throbbed, spilling its cold light down. Its voices on this plane, the Spittle and the Sigh, felt the shifting need of their Most Holy and left the repurposing chamber. The stairs creaked under the weight of their bodies, the gristle, bone, and tooth combined and animated for a greater will. Black cloaks dyed with ichor rested upon their shoulders, the edges trailing behind them. Long had the two watched the earth from their prison in the lower realm, watched and learned and seethed. For countless eons, they had been the only two entities of their entire world with independent thought, and only given these forms when the barriers had grown weak.

They were tasked to prepare the way for the Ovessa, the Serpentine Star of Glistening Light. A demi-god of its own particular corner of one of the gutter realms, it held sway over all of its creation. And like all hungry tyrants, it wanted more. Earth was so free, so diverse, it was indeed enticing with its blasphemous existence.

While other things from myriad quarters of the gutter realms found the earth a curiosity and may have used the weakening of the barriers to explore it, the Ovessa orchestrated a full-scale invasion. It considered it a right. It considered the earth's very existence as justification.

And so the Spittle and the Sigh went to the top floor of the hotel, to the room that used to be a ballroom. There, in the ceiling, where reality was ripping itself apart, the cold light was brightest. There, flesh heaved and undulated, slick with pus. Coiled muscle, pink and hairless, prepared to bend. Only part of that other realm was visible through the portal, only part of a sky made of viscera. Through that hole to another realm, the light gleamed down, bathing its Voices, filling them with its need.

"The Crimsonata has arrived," said the Sigh.

"Let us see an end to this," said the Spittle.

"All in honor of the Ovessa," said the Sigh.

CHAPTER 38

Car doors slammed and echoed through the empty town. Elliot parked in front of a library at random, not sure where else to go. The place was empty, no people anywhere. Everyone had noticed the effect of the light in Eldridge, grey and soft. It washed out all the colors, like a filter app for pictures on your phone. It made everyone as uneasy as did the silence.

Hayden and Roma geared up like they were ready for war. Each had a gun belt holding two pistols, and a row of extra clips, along with a pouch of bullets. They had a string of shells to go with the shotguns over their shoulders, accompanying the machete. That was in addition to the various other small knives concealed all over them, along with collapsible batons, handcuffs, and brass knuckles.

"Where are we supposed to go?" asked Elliot.

"I honestly don't know," replied Binici. "Timothy never got back to me. He's here somewhere, hopefully."

That answer didn't sit well with Elliot. None of this did. He was trying his hardest to support Audrey, to believe in her, but it was taking a lot.

The five of them walked up the middle of the street, taking it all in. A paint store with displays in the window sat next to a bank with tall stone pillars. A placard sat outside on the sidewalk announcing a financing plan. There was a small café called Doc's that looked to serve mostly sandwiches. Elliot noticed what appeared to be blood on the windows and smears on the floor. He pointed it out to Roma who frowned.

He hadn't noticed it at first, until they had started walking, but the air felt strange. Oily, and thick. Like it was leaving behind a residue. He wiped two fingers against his skin and rubbed them together. Nothing came off, but he could still feel if there.

"Maybe we should knock on some of these doors?" Elliot mused out loud.

"Go right ahead," said Roma. "I don't think you're going to get an answer."

Elliot pounded on the door of a lawyer's office and waited for a moment before trying again. It was the middle of a Wednesday afternoon, people should be there. People should be everywhere.

"They're all hiding," said Binici.

"They're all dead," said Hayden.

"Or worse," added Audrey.

They came to another bank and Elliot tried the door. It was unlocked. He walked inside, Audrey calling out his name behind him. Ignoring her, he kept moving through the second set of double doors into the interior of the bank. It was completely open, just like a normal business day, except it was free from customers or workers. No one. Roma and Audrey came in behind him, looking around.

"Anybody ever want to rob a bank, because this is your chance."

"We shouldn't be confined like this," said Roma.

"Let me just look really quick," said Elliot.

He swept through the bank, going behind the tellers' windows and back into the offices. He even peeked into the vault, its door standing wide open. No signs of anyone, not a drop of blood. Nothing even knocked over. It was like they had simply got up and walked away.

"Okay," he said, returning to them. "Let's go."

"What were you looking for?" asked Audrey.

"I don't know, clues?"

"We're not the Scooby Gang, Elliot."

He frowned and walked away from her. Audrey seemed to think that she had to carry this all on herself, but she was wrong. He was here to shoulder some of the burden; that was part of being a sibling. He wanted to help and wanted to prove it.

More blocks passed.

Elliot was staring up at a clinic window when a shape darted across the road, someone bundled up in a long brown jacket.

"Hey!" Roma yelled, before giving chase.

Everyone followed, turning down a side street. The jacket was discarded on the ground, a member of the Invocated standing there.

Without hesitation, Hayden pulled his gun and fired into the thing three times. It fell, and he fired twice more into its head. He immediately ejected his clip and began to reload it from his pouch. He didn't finish in time, as two more crawled out from behind the dumpster.

"Back out onto the main road!" yelled Roma, firing on the other two.

They ran back out onto the street only to find hundreds of the Invocated waiting for them. Hayden kept firing, trying to take as many of them as he could. His eyes were wild, wide, and glazed over. Shot after shot, death and death. The blackest blood sprayed everywhere around them. Mindlessly, pointlessly. There were still hundreds more. Finally, Roma reached over and grabbed his hand while he was clicking on empty and lowered it.

"They're not even attacking, Alec."

"They must all die!" he snarled.

"And they will," she said quietly. "But not that way."

Encircled by the Invocated, they simply stood there and stared at them. In the bizarre light, Elliot was really able to examine them. Stripped of identifying features, they all looked nearly identical in their hideousness. The white rags hung from their bodies in tatters, showing enough sickening flesh to reveal where some may have once been male or female. They were neither now, inhuman creatures forged in some aberrant flame. Swaying back and forth, they began to part, making way for the five to move forward.

"What's happening?" asked Binici, clutching onto Audrey's arm.

"They're herding us," said Roma.

"Where?" asked Elliot.

"We'll find out," said the member of the Wall.

CHAPTER 39

The Wiltshire Hotel. It rose up, squat and dark, like a blot on the skyline. The brick exterior had taken on a perpetual dampness, one that left it discolored and looking bruised. The windows were covered with a grime collected from elsewhere, clinging in random, abstract patterns. The awnings and gutters were beginning to rust, flaking off in particles. The painted trim peeled and curled, revealing rotting wood beneath.

The Wiltshire was being consumed by the Ovessa as it made its way further into the earth realm, a first stop on its way toward the rest of the world.

Audrey could feel the disease permeating the building. It was apparent. She could tell the others felt it, too. The looks on their faces said it all. This was the epicenter of the invasion, the madness. The infection had taken root here.

Still, the Invocated had not attacked. They stood almost ten paces away from her and the others, swaying. Audrey stood on the sidewalk before the stairs to the hotel, staring up at it. She didn't know what to do. Were her secret magic powers supposed to kick in now? Nothing was happening besides her being terrified.

Two figured stepped out of the shadows above them, coming from the doors of the hotel. Dressed in black cloaks, she couldn't make much of them out. Then they flung back their robes and Audrey wished they hadn't. Fully formed humanoids, they looked built from pieces of bone, talon, and gristle. Ink flowed from their head instead of hair.

"Little interlopers, the end to your adventure has come," said the male.

"He is the Spittle as I am the Sigh. We are the voices of the Most Holy, your new divine, the Ovessa."

"Uh, what?" said Elliot.

"Your understanding is irrelevant, only your obliteration. Obliteration or supplication are the only avenues, but you have not the latter choice."

"Option C," growled Hayden, reaching for his guns.

"So predictable," said the Spittle. "So be it. Allow us to grant you an audience with our latest creation. You may find oblivion through it, knowing your battle was mighty, yet still pointless."

As the Spittle and the Sigh parted at the top of the stairs, Audrey began to lose her cool. This wasn't how she saw things playing out. She didn't even have a weapon with which to battle a monster.

"Inanis!" she hissed under her breath.

"It is the way of things in this realm for objects to have names. We are still growing accustomed to that and have not named our newest spawn yet," said the Spittle.

The Sigh smiled. "However, we believe 'The Sanctified' is appropriate."

An enormous man walked out of the hotel doors. Audrey did a double take and realized it was no man. Over seven feet of rippling muscle, with blistered pink skin, it only had three fingers on each hand and hoofed feet. A scar ran down the center of its chest, separating two rows of nipples. An abomination blossomed at its groin. By far the worst was its head, or where its head should be. A shuddering, shifting, melting maw of chaos. Something like a choking roar came out of that semi-corporeal mass.

"That was Timothy Faure, by the way," said Mr. Inanis, appearing behind Audrey and making her scream.

"Oh Timothy, no!" wailed Binici.

The Sigh waved her hand dismissively. "It doesn't matter how many of you there are, you will all die by the Ovessa's will."

As the Sanctified made its way down the steps, Hayden and Roma readied their weapons. Binici clutched onto Audrey and Elliot looked around for a weapon. Audrey turned to look up at Inanis, who appeared bored.

"You said you had a plan!"

"I do. Give it a second."

Audrey wondered how she had made it to this point in her life. Part of her wasn't surprised, in a way. Her life hadn't exactly been normal. She had been a lot of things, made a lot of mistakes, but at least when she went out, she could say she tried. Maybe she didn't battle monsters like her favorite super heroes, but she could play her role.

Roma started firing at the thing that had been Faure. The Sanctified. Audrey wished she could be more like Roma. Self-confident and driven. A badass. She had never even fired a gun in her life, not that she really wanted to. Still, it was the idea of it. The idea of being the protector. Ellen Ripley and Buffy Summers and Wonder Woman. The heroines of movies, books, and comics had always been her inspiration and here was one in real life.

Her life had been lived through a computer screen. Lived vicariously through the exploits of fictional characters. Anything that came too close to the real world had made her nervous, anxious, paranoid. Sometimes causing bouts of agoraphobia. Audrey didn't feel like any of that had really changed, but damn if she didn't have a different perspective now. Life had always been loud and messy and cruel, but watching Roma take a step back to reload, it could also be just as noble and bold and epic.

As much as it scared her, that's what she wanted. No more hiding, no more playing it safe.

"Inanis!" she yelled at him.

"Yep, you're ready. Let's go."

And time stopped.

CHAPTER 40

"What just happened?" asked Audrey, glancing around.

Binici still held onto to her, looking equally startled. Everything was frozen in place except for them and Inanis.

"A sort of 'time snap,' but it won't last for long and will begin to break down once we're inside the building. We need to go now," he said.

He made his way around the Sanctified and toward the steps. Binici went to reach out a hand toward the thing that used to be Faure, then thought better of it. They hurried to catch up with the man in the suit. He stood between the two cloaked voices of the Ovessa on the landing, waiting for them. Nodding at them, he led them inside.

A few more of the Invocated stood immobile inside, staring off into nothingness. the Ovessa's taint had affected the interior of the building more rapidly, signs of degradation more apparent. The walls bowed, the paint discolored in large splotches. The trim splintered in places, rotting out. Patches of the ceiling had collapsed, littering the floor with debris. Parts of the floor looked ready to fall in, too. The thick, oily feel to the air was worse here, like you were swimming through it. It smelled of burnt motor oil and spent sex. Too pungent to ignore.

"We need to make it to the fourth floor," whispered Inanis.

Audrey nodded. She wasn't entirely sure what was happening, but it was better than facing down monsters while defenseless outside. She started to take the steps up when she realized that Binici had let go of her hand. Turning to look for the old woman, she spied her peering into a back room.

"What are you doing?" hissed Audrey. "Let's go."

"It's some kind of assembly line, I think. And the creatures in here defy reason!"

"That's great, worry about it later."

"I'm sorry," said Binici. "This is all just..."

Her sentence was cut short by a tentacle whipping out from beyond the doorway and piercing through her lower abdomen.

"No!" screamed Audrey, rushing down the steps.

"We don't have time for this," remarked Inanis, throwing out a gesture and burning the squid-like creature who had come lurching out of the room.

Audrey skidded down next to where Binici had collapsed. A chunk of the tentacle was still squirming inside, staunching most of the blood leak. She was in terrible pain. Her hands reached down to the wound and came away trembling.

"I'm sorry, I'm sorry," Binici kept saying over and over again.

"It's okay, Inanis can help you, right?"

"They're alerted to our presence now. I can either save her or take us to the Ovessa so you can save us all, Audrey," he said.

"God damn it," said Audrey, hugging onto the professor.

"Audrey, this was always about you. Go, please."

"I won't leave you here."

"She doesn't have to stay here," said Inanis. "Stealth isn't a factor anymore."

With his index finger held high above him, he motioned in a circle and then clapped his hands. Audrey felt weightless and saw colors bleed together. Everything jumbled for a moment. Space realigned and they were in another room, somewhere large. Audrey made the mistake of looking up.

Reality was shattering, a septic hole seeping light out into the room. Up in the ceiling, something luminous and fleshy throbbed against our world. Serpentine yet bulbous, its almost reflective surface glistened with diseased intent. Emanating malevolence. Audrey could feel it trying to coat her psyche, could feel it whispering to her, seducing her.

Oh, how the Ovessa needs! Needs to gather its children and make them whole, make them unified. Doesn't Audrey feel the constant burden of doubt, the burden of choice? Only those plagued by identity must suffer like that. Only those shackled with free will must be forced to endure. The Ovessa offers bliss, offers sanctuary in its light. Here there is but one will, one purpose. All is one.

Above, the Ovessa lunged and swelled, growing slicker with its dew. It was a whole world made cognizant, a god made matter. It believed in its right because it was all it had ever known, except for those heretics it had watched through the barrier. Who was there to tell it otherwise?

The Ovessa neeeeeds! Needs to be more, needs to be pure. Doesn't Audrey need? Doesn't Audrey need to let go of fear and pain, of sadness and anger? Embrace and begin the truth, begin the future. Begin being better.

Being better...

Inanis touched her shoulder and snapped her out of it.

"It's scared of you, knows what you are," he said.

"It tried to get in my head," said Audrey, gripping her skull.

"Tried that with everyone."

She shook Binici, the old woman had passed out beside her. "C'mon, please don't be dead."

"What, what happened?"

"Are you okay?"

She reached down and gingerly touched the piece of tentacle still in her abdomen. It wasn't twitching anymore but her fingers still came away bloody. Binici smiled up at Audrey as best she could. Despite everything, Audrey had grown fond of the professor and didn't want to see anything else happen to her.

The Ovessa began to seize and twitch high above them, the glistening light growing brighter.

Inanis turned to her. "Audrey, I need you to flow as the Crimsonata, here in the room, right now."

CHAPTER 41

"**W**here the fuck did Audrey go?" screamed Elliot.

One minute they were all standing there, the next minute her, Binici, and Inanis were gone. He didn't like that at all. Not only was it creepy, he didn't like her disappearing on him. Not that he could do much to protect her from all of this. He didn't even have a weapon.

The Invocated still stood around them in a silent circle, but the thing called the Sanctified was still approaching and nothing Roma and Hayden shot at him seemed to be slowing him down. He really wished he had a weapon, a gun or a baseball bat. He'd take a steak knife at this point.

"The Crimsonata has fled," said the Spittle.

"Their folly," said the Sigh. "Pitiful human conjurings in an attempt to hide within the building. Either our brethren will find them or the Ovessa will see to them in its own glory."

Roma had ditched her handguns in exchange for her shotgun. That did more damage, knocking the beast backwards. Elliot swooped in and picked up a discarded gun, yelling for some ammo. In one fluid motion, she dropped a clip to the ground, while continuing to fire the shotgun. He fumbled to load the gun, having no idea what he was doing.

Taking a cue from Roma, Hayden switched to his shotgun as well. The blasts knocked the Sanctified back, Hayden growing bold. Roma yelled at him to move, but he ignored her.

"Filth will always be put down!" Hayden roared, eyes wide. "Down to the ground!"

The Sanctified reached up, taking a blast full the chest in the process, and reached past the shotgun. It gripped Hayden's right arm and snapped it in half.

Hayden screamed in agony, breaking free of the creature. His shotgun slid back to Elliot who picked it up. Hayden staggered, his bone ripping out of his skin. The Sanctified regained his footing and came forward. Instead of a massive blow, it grabbed Hayden by the shoulders with both hands and held him in place.

"Burn, burn them all!" bellowed Hayden. "Suffer not a..."

The Sanctified lowered its swirling, jittering mess of a head onto Hayden's head, silencing him, engulfing him. When the creature raised back up, the Promethean Wall member's head was gone, a bloody stump all that remained.

To his left, he heard Roma whisper, "Goodbye Alec, I hope you find peace."

The Sanctified seemed to forget about them for the moment as it busied itself with devouring the rest Hayden's body, starting on the broken arm. Elliot watched in horror as the arm passed into the glitching, tumbling mass. He wondered if that was to be his own fate.

"Tell me I've loaded this gun right," he said to Roma.

She looked it over. "You did it right."

"I'm sorry about Hayden."

Roma shrugged. "I had a feeling his end was coming anyway."

Elliot looked up to the two on the porch. "Why are you doing this anyhow?"

The female looked down at him and gave him something like a smile.

"Why does anything grow and evolve? Because that is the way of things. Even you, here and now, serve a purpose. You test our Sanctified, prove its worth. See if its properties are functioning as they should be."

"Properties? To maim and kill? Yeah, I think you've got a winner."

"The Sanctified does not consume to nourish itself. We are all part of a greater whole. That which it takes into itself is matter transmuted unto the horde, meat repurposed in honor of the Ovessa."

"Wait," said Roma. "His body is used to build monsters?"

The Sigh and the Spittle both smiled wide.

Roma began laughing, far too hard for the given situation, as far as Elliot was concerned.

"What the hell?" he asked.

"Ah Hayden, you prick," she said, slinging her gun over her back as she watched the Sanctified start in on his legs. "You'd be so pissed."

CHAPTER 42

"Y ou want me to do what?"

Inanis turned and threw out his hand, a stray Invocated that had wandered into the room burst into flame. Back to Audrey, he frowned. For a moment, she thought he was going to yell at her, but instead he took a deep, measured breath.

"You need to take off your clothes, right here, right now. Walk beneath the Ovessa, and flow. Do what you were always meant to do."

But, but," stammered Audrey. "I have no idea how to! And why here?"

"The Outer Gods have always fed upon the Crimsonata because they didn't have anything else tastier. But if they get a whiff of the Ovessa while dining on you? Let's just say I'm willing to bet their palates will evolve."

Another Invocated rushed into the room and exploded into smoldering ash at the gesture of the man in the suit. Audrey stared up at the oozing god world and wondered at the plan. Could it be as simple as that?

"Try, dear," came Binici's weak voice from the floor beside her.

"I don't know how," she whispered back.

"Yes you do, you've always known how," said Inanis. "Don't worry about the clothes, just go!"

Audrey walked farther out into the room, farther beneath the Ovessa. The slick sheen of pus along its skin gleamed, muscles taunt and expectant. The hole revealed that portion of the Ovessa in this realm was crumbling, reality breaking apart between this world and its own. Eventually all of the Ovessa would be here, a world made of flesh and able to remake the earth as it saw fit. It undulated in pleasure, flexing its might.

Literally, this was what Audrey Darrow was born to do. To keep things like this at bay. To protect this world from monsters. Not to feed gods, but this. She took hold of that thought and concentrated on that.

She thought about her mother, frazzled and lost, following pieces of a doctrine she didn't fully understand. She thought about all those women throughout history who had flowed to protect the earth from this moment. She thought about herself standing here now, facing off against a petty god that wanted to enslave her planet.

These thoughts coalesced, and Audrey thought about her last dream.

High above, the Ovessa began to buck and thrust.

The orb of black ichor. The blood of divinity made eons ago and stored on a plane elsewhere. A supply that would never run out, its contents purified once ran through the body of the Crimsonata. Through her magic. More than just food, so much more. Celestial essence, distilled down, marking the bodies of those who wielded it as something more. But it had always been more than just food.

Audrey had begun to float, and she hadn't even realized it.

From that greater realm, that was not really a desert, the essence came to her. Flew to her. It had been called by the Crimsonata. She did not bleed her own blood, but the blood forged for her by cosmic juggernauts, primordial beings who had engineered the universe. The blood poured into her from the far, unseen realm, and she understood.

The Crimsonata had survived for millennia because they were a weapon, too.

The black blood began to seep out of every pore of Audrey's body as she floated in the air, diffusing through her skin. It soaked into her clothing, but that didn't matter. She had control. Above her, the Ovessa let out a high-pitched noise, something like a psychic squeal that shook the room. It tried to push itself through the hole, squeezing its bulk further into the earth realm. Reality splintered around the aperture as quickly as the roof itself. Audrey continued floating and bleeding, appraising the god.

Images flashed in her mind of all those women in the desert. All those women who had been the Crimsonata before her. A part of them all now resides within the essence, guarding it for all eternity. They look at her as one. As one, they gave her their love, their support, their strength. Audrey saw her mother. She saw her pride.

With that, Audrey hurled the blood from her body up at the Ovessa, firing it like liquid projectiles. When it hit, it didn't just splatter, but pierced the diseased skin. The world god howled again, thrashing. She threw more blood, a bigger discharge that she balled up in her hands like a baseball. It blew a hole deep into the Ovessa's hide. As she did this, droplets of blood were drifting from her body and floating up above her, vaporizing into atoms. She failed to notice most of these until one drop lifted from the end of her nose. She paused, watching it slowly soar away, and was almost cut in half by a blast of light from the Ovessa.

Audrey tumbled to the floor. While the ichor was still coating her clothing, it was almost entirely gone from her body. Had she used it all up? From the sensations she had received during the dream experience, the source was endless. The Ovessa creased its skin and shot out another bolt of light across the room, its aim off by a good five feet. She'd become the Crimsonata, but she'd accomplished nothing.

Suddenly, the entire ceiling above them grew dark, as if it no longer existed. A galactic vista overtook the space above them, one vast and dark, yet filled with movement. The presence in that deeper black weighed down on Audrey, filled her with a terrible dread, and forced her to look away. These were entities far beyond the Ovessa, beings that had both created the Crimsonata, and also created other universes. She felt their concentration bear down upon her, examining her.

They turned their attention toward the Ovessa.

Another psychic shriek as the Outer Gods drew closer. It tried to pull away from its hole in the roof, but a new feast had been found. An Invocated staggered in but fell and began to liquefy before Inanis could even set it on fire.

"Well, this has worked out much like I expected," he said.

CHAPTER 43

A s Inanis spoke, the Spittle and the Sigh rushed into the room.

"Most Holy, no!" screamed the Sigh.

"What have you done?" bellowed the Spittle.

"Work of the Outer Gods," replied Inanis, pointing up.

The hole was starting to close, reality starting to repair itself. The Ovessa was being dragged back to its own world from where the deeper black could feed on it forever. Its voices must have seen this and ran for their disappearing god.

"We're coming, Most Holy We will never abandon you!"

A last beam of light enveloped them before the hole closed. For a moment, the greater, vast darkness lay above them, and Audrey feared what was to become of her. Would they still want her to be the Crimsonata? Was she just to walk away or were they simply going to kill her now that they no longer had a use for her? Now that their gaze was turning back to her, she could barely stand it. It felt like gravity had increased, but in her psyche as well as her body. She was powerless against their whims and she knew it. Such a lack of control was utterly terrifying.

Their attention shifted.

"Yeah, I've got this," said Inanis.

And the ceiling went back to normal.

Audrey gawked at Inanis. "What the fuck was that?"

"Right now, you'd better see to Emily."

Audrey glanced over and saw the old woman bleeding out. The tentacle was gone.

"What happened?" Audrey asked, scrambling over.

"When the Ovessa was transported back to its realm, all of its creations went with it."

Audrey cradled Binici's head in her lap. "It'll be okay, we'll..."

"I got to see you flow," whispered the professor. "You were glorious."

"I was the Crimsonata," said Audrey, surprised at her tears. "I saw the line of my lineage, millions of women, and the never-ending source of the blood. It was created by the Outer Gods themselves and we were the conduits. But it wasn't just food, never just food."

"Audrey," said Inanis.

"The blood was always meant to be more, whatever the Crimsonata needed to it be. To kill, to heal, to protect, to lead. We made the blood into that. We found our own divinity in the blood."

"Audrey," Inanis said a little more forcefully.

She looked down. Binici was dead. Audrey sighed.

"Hold on, I'm just going to teleport us."

"Why didn't you..."

They were outside next to Roma and Elliot.

"... do that earlier?"

"Couldn't show my hand," said Inanis with a shrug.

"You're alive!" exclaimed Elliot, coming over to give his sister a hug. "What happened?"

"I became the Crimsonata, beat up the bad guy, and sorta saved the day. You?"

"Roma mostly saved my ass until everything disappeared. Oh, and Hayden died."

Audrey shrugged. She wasn't heartbroken over that news. "Binici died."

"Sorry."

"Yeah."

Roma sat down on the steps to the hotel and rubbed her

temples. "I'm honestly surprised any of us survived this. I'm surprised this whole thing worked!"

Inanis waved his hand. "Nah, I knew it would work. We haven't been satisfied with the Crimsonata in centuries, but nobody wanted to be bothered to change the status quo. I simply took some initiative."

Audrey slowly backed away from Inanis. "What are you saying?"

"I'm one of the Outer Gods. What, you thought my name was actually "Inanis?" Inanis is just your Latin word for empty. I thought that was funny considering the circumstances."

"But the barriers," stammered Audrey. "The blood that keeps you back!"

"Audrey, we can do whatever we want, whenever we want. That was just the myth to keep you all flowing. A bit of propaganda. Granted, it was true the barriers *would* break down, but that has nothing to do with us. Well, it did. That was our fault for making the Crimsonata in the first place."

"What?" asked Roma.

"Audrey gets it. She draws her blood from a higher plane. And that blood has to be constantly drawn now to keep a wall there. An unforeseen side effect. We really weren't paying much attention when we threw this project together."

"Are you serious?" asked Audrey, floored.

"Hey, I saw all the flaws in the plan. So I saw that a need would arise, something that would force the others to go along with change. No Crimsonata for twenty years. I waited until there was only one Crimsonata left on the planet with a young daughter who didn't know any better. And then I saw to it that your mother died in car crash. I've orchestrated this whole thing since you were seven years old."

Audrey reared back and punched him in the face.

Inanis just laughed.

"I think this whole thing has worked out splendidly for everyone."

"Thousands of people are dead!" Roma yelled.

"Well, we *are* gods after all," Inanis replied with a smile.

And he vanished.

"Mother fucker," said Elliot, staring at the spot where he had been standing.

"So are you still the Crimsonata?" asked Roma.

"I don't know," said Audrey. "The Outer Gods don't need me anymore, so I don't have to flow. The way Inanis talked, the connection would be severed. Chances are, I was the last."

"Jesus," said Elliot. "I guess we just go home."

Home. What was home now? Sitting alone in a small apartment, hiding behind the internet. She had seen behind the curtain, looked at the hidden face of the universe. How could she go back to that life after facing down gods and monsters? She might not be the Crimsonata anymore, but she remembered the sensation. She knew what her lineage was. The blood had flowed through her, albeit only once, but it had been enough.

"I need to talk to Roma first," said Audrey. "I have some decisions to make."

CHAPTER 44

FOURTEEN MONTHS LATER

This summer had been just had humid as the previous one, but it was at last winding down. It was the tail end of August and Audrey was sitting in a car sipping coffee with Roma. Twilight was settling on the state park whose name she couldn't remember. She was lucky that she could recall they were in Utah.

The scenery was beautiful. The trees were lush with greenery and the rocks large and ancient. The sun cut ribbons of colors across the sky as it dipped below the horizon. Too bad they weren't here for the sights.

"Hey, it's about nine o'clock," said Roma.

"I know," said Audrey.

Roma wasn't overbearing, she just knew they were on a timetable. Audrey could appreciate that. She placed her coffee in the cup holder and fished through the satchel at her feet. Two different pill bottles, one for little whites, one for little reds. They helped combat her depression and anxiety, made her a better Audrey, the her she was supposed to be. She slipped the pills into her mouth and swallowed them down with coffee.

So much had changed.

Thousands upon thousands of dead, mutilated, and missing in towns across America. The authorities had tried to piece it all together, but it hadn't made much sense. Terrorists were blamed, of course. The Promethean Wall was behind the scenes ensuring that. Eventually new tragedies had taken over the media's attention and only the conspiracy theorist still anguished over what had happened last summer.

Audrey was one of the few who knew the truth and it haunted her still. She agonized over her choices that led up to the standoff at the hotel in Eldridge. A lot of that was what led her to now.

It wasn't time yet, so they sat in the car a while longer. She knew the game plan, so there was no reason to go over it with Roma again. She liked that Roma didn't need to talk all the time, didn't need to be talked to. Oh, they could definitely babble when the time came, but it wasn't a necessity. Audrey had realized a few months back that the other woman was her best friend and it had almost made her cry. She'd never had one before. She wondered if that made them better partners or if it was more of a liability.

After the events at Eldridge, Ohio, she had joined the Promethean Wall. She had seen what was possible, of what the darkness was capable. It was time to give back, to do something more than just for herself. At first, she figured the people in charge would just laugh at her, some girl with no skills who had once been the kind of thing they hunted. But the Council had been intrigued by her story, though they had never actually met. Roma spoke on her behalf, telling them how she no longer was the Crimsonata but had seen the threat firsthand. The Council had believed in her and her intentions, giving Roma a year to train her and get her up to speed on everything.

They lived in a house in Cleveland, not far from Eldridge, so they could observe the site in case there were any lingering effects. Roma trained her in martial arts and weaponry. Krav Maga, Silat, Kung Fu. Throwing daggers, long blades, and marksmanship with handguns, rifles, and shotguns. It was hard training during long days, but Audrey found herself growing more proficient in all of it. The Wall had been the ones to pay for her prescriptions, too.

The women traveled, went on simple missions. They killed a Chupacabra that had strayed too far north and managed to take down an Aswang lurking in a graveyard. Audrey began to feel confident in her new role. She began to actually believe she might belong standing next to Roma.

A lot had come to light over the past year. It turned out that Hayden had been engaged in a lot of unsanctioned missions, killing things off the books that he wasn't supposed to. The Council had wanted to bring in two other teams to assist on "The Crimsonata event," but he had played down the importance. Had he survived, he would have likely lost his cell, if not been struck from the Wall entirely. The women never did find out what had happened to him to make him the way he was, but in the end, it didn't matter. Perhaps even stranger was what Audrey discovered about Emily Binici. The old woman had left everything in her will to Audrey. She had a house in California just waiting for her. She still didn't know what to do about that.

Elliot wasn't pleased with her decision, to put it mildly. He felt like, after escaping certain doom, why jump willingly back into it? It's not that he didn't trust Roma, he just didn't trust the Wall as a whole. Didn't get why Audrey would want to risk her life. She tried to explain it to him in Eldridge that day and had tried on the phone countless times since then. She eventually had to tell him that she'd stop taking his calls if he didn't drop the subject. That had shut him up.

Soon Roma and she would be set up as another cell. Possibly still in Cleveland, probably in another city. She'd even thought about offering to base it out of Binici's house. They'd stay together and take on a third, and likely a fourth person. Tonight was Audrey's last training mission.

"So, werewolves, huh," said Audrey. "Who knew?"

Roma snorted out a laugh. "Yeah, I was surprised, too. But these aren't the romance novel type werewolves, more like the baby-eating type. Savage beasts that only want to hunt and gorge on human flesh."

"Lovely. You really know how to make graduation day memorable."

"You'll do fine, Audrey. You're prepared for this. You're more skilled at one year in than I was by far."

Audrey smiled. "Thanks, Allison."

"C'mon, sun is down," said Roma, draining the last of her coffee. "Let's check weapons and go."

Audrey climbed out and walked to the trunk. Popping it open, she began to retrieve her gear. Handguns, shotgun, knives, collapsible baton, handcuffs, machete, she looked ready to go to war. She was in a way. War against those things that slipped through the cracks, that disappeared into the shadows. War against the things that ruined lives and got away with it.

Audrey checked her gun and looked up at Roma. "Let's go bag some werewolves."

CHAPTER 45

They moved into the woods, separating, but staying within sight of each other. A lot of preparation and research had gone into this mission. There was a lot of disinformation about werewolves out there.

They only hunted on the nights before, during, and directly after a full moon. The rest of the time they were normal people. But they couldn't control the beast within them, couldn't control the ravenous hunger and need to slaughter. A werewolf would kill animals, but it preferred humans, and any human that survived a bite was forever transformed. Any weapon could injure it, but like the legends said, they were deathly allergic to silver, so that helped with putting them down for good. That or magic.

Weapons hadn't been a problem. As soon as they had been tapped for this case, they had requisitioned the appropriate supplies. The Wall's armory had sent specialized bullets and blades, all field tested against this particular threat. The biggest problem had been tracking the creatures. They were already into their second month, second night. Roma felt confident that the werewolves were lurking in the park, it was just a matter of finding them. However, their failure from last month to even engage the creatures ate away at both of them. It was time to be done with this.

Sweeping the landscape with a flashlight in one hand, a gun braced in the other, Audrey looked for any signs of movement. There had been a murder not far from here last night, a trucker pulled from his cab and butchered. Examining the map and pinpointing the other kill sites, all bets were on the park. Audrey ducked under a low branch and swung her light back behind her. She was on a narrow trail, following its meandering path as she took it deeper into the forest. So far there wasn't a sign.

Roma was about twenty yards off in the trees, moving almost silently through the brush. She had a smaller light, one more to help Audrey keep track of her than to detect any clues. They needed to stay close, but not too close. Kill patterns and drag marks led Roma to speculate that there were three of the creatures out here. They might not attack if they viewed the women as a united threat.

Despite the situation, Audrey felt good. She felt alive. Something about tonight made her feel vibrant and energetic. She believed in the Promethean Wall, the group that Roma had unveiled to her as opposed to the one Hayden wanted it to be. She knew she could do good, protect people. She was glad that Roma was far enough away that she couldn't see the smile pulling at the corners of her mouth. Audrey couldn't figure out why she was feeling like this.

"Get it together," she whispered to herself.

The trail sloped down, and Audrey took the few feet without trouble. The trees here were sparse, the underbrush thick. Thin oaks rose up to create a partial canopy, the basin full of vines, saplings, and shrubs. Some small critter scurried off as her light passed over it. The trail all but vanished and remerged on the other side where the ground rose again.

"Audrey, let's..." began Roma.

A werewolf burst out from the underbrush.

Without hesitation, Roma raised her gun and began firing. Three shots, four. It didn't want to go down and it was still moving. Audrey aimed her own gun and fired. Her bullets spun the creature, Roma putting a final bullet in its head when it came to fall at her feet.

Audrey heard a sound behind her. Turning, she pulled the shotgun off her back. The Werewolf rose up above her, a full seven feet tall. It was covered in greasy dark brown fur and reeked of musk. Walking on padded feet, with long clawed hands, its head sat squat on it shoulders with long ears and a pointed snout. Sickly, yellow eyes peered down at her and drool dripped from its muzzle.

She regarded it for a full three seconds before squeezing the trigger on her shotgun and blowing out its stomach. The creature howled and stumbled back. She racked the gun and fired again. Its abdomen was obliterated. The werewolf lay there twitching and bleeding out. She heard a blast behind her. Spinning, she saw Roma taking out the third one.

"Hand guns are shit," called Roma. "Give them a shot to the head to be sure."

Audrey stepped up to the werewolf. It was already changing back to human form. She didn't want to see that; didn't want to see who it was the rest of the time when it wasn't a monster. She put the barrel to its face and pulled the trigger. The gore splattered back onto her legs.

Handguns nearly useless and shotguns spent, she began walking back over to Roma. She didn't feel bad about what she had to do. These people had been infected with something they couldn't control, and they were killing innocent people. There was no cure, no containment. There was only the Wall.

Audrey was a few paces away from Roma, watching the woman wipe blood from her face with her arm, when the fourth werewolf attacked. It had sprung out of nowhere, soundless until it was upon Roma. It hurled her to the ground, holding her down. Claws dug into her left shoulder, she screamed as it reared back. To maim, to kill.

Audrey saw all of this in a span of a few seconds.

And Audrey reacted.

She screamed with all the rage of thousands of women, all the strength of her lineage. She hurled out her hands and the blood went as she commanded it. Sharp and black, the eternal ichor. It tore through the werewolf, dozens of knives propelled by willpower. Not only did her flechettes mutilate, her blood was a greater poison than the silver ever could be. Because she had willed it so. The werewolf was dead before it toppled off Roma to the ground.

Roma fumbled back away from the corpse, gawking up at Audrey. "What... What?"

Audrey, tears running down her face, watched as the blood of the Crimsonata settled back down into her skin.

CHAPTER 46

Back at the motel, Audrey sat on the bed while Roma went and got a shower. Audrey thought her partner was being extraordinarily calm about all of this. She lifted her hand and let the blood drift up, solidifying into the shape of an orb. Audrey had no idea how she knew how to do this. It was like she had suddenly tapped into the memories of all the past Crimsonata. A lot of it was still hazy, but the basics were there.

The thing that bothered her was *why*. Why now? Was it just because Roma had been in danger? She hoped so. But what would that mean for her in the Wall. This was her life now.

Roma came out of the bathroom in shorts and a bra, holding a towel to her shoulder. She was wincing, and the towel was turning red. She swayed a bit getting to the bed.

"I think we might need more than the regular med kit," she said.

"Let me see," said Audrey.

Roma grimaced as she pulled away the towel. It was bad. The werewolf had dug his claw in pretty deep, it would require more than just stitches.

"Do you trust me?" Audrey asked.

"What?"

"Do you trust me?"

Roma nodded, biting her lip.

Audrey brought up her hands and called forth the blood. She willed it smooth and gentle, soft and loving. The blood of the matron, the blood of the nurse. It slipped inside Roma and began to reshape her wound, to bind it back together. Roma's eyes fluttered as the black blood healed her, making her warm.

Then it was done.

"Okay," said Audrey.

Roma moved her arm, staring at it. "How did you do that?"

"I don't know, I just knew how to. Just like at the park."

"So you're the Crimsonata again?"

"I guess. Maybe I have been this whole time."

"But why now?"

"You're my best friend, Allison," whispered Audrey.

Roma put her arm around Audrey. "You are truly the most remarkable person I've ever met, Audrey Darrow. I mean that. You're not going to lose me."

"You can't promise that. And I might lose everything once the Wall finds out I'm the Crimsonata again."

'They knew you were before and didn't care. Hell, that was a selling point to them. You just finished all of your training *without* any special powers. Now you have them again. You might fit in more than you think."

Audrey flopped back onto the bed. "The Wall aside, why did I get my powers back? Was it just being scared for you? Are the Outer Gods back for me? Did the Ovessa break free again? Some other unknown scenario?"

Roma went across the room to her suitcase and slipped on a T-shirt. She stood there for a second, with her long dark hair still damp, and considered Audrey's words. A look crossed her face, but she shook her head.

"What?" asked Audrey.

"Well, you used to dream stuff, right? Maybe some answers will come to you that way again?"

"Maybe," said Audrey, looking unconvinced.

"You weren't in control before. You are now."

Audrey sat up in the bed. "Actually, you're right. Hold on a sec."

"Wait, what are you..."

Audrey crossed her legs on the bed and closed her eyes.

The endless desert. Warm and humid, smelling of incense. The sky isn't blue, more a purple, or reddish-brown. Faint wisps of clouds, but no sun in the sky. The illumination comes from elsewhere here. The always twilight of stars almost visible, perhaps, twinkling too large in their heavens.

The orb is always flowing, never ending, a galactic droplet. It casts no shadow, for it has no weight, no gravity, nothing but a presence which envelops this entire realm. This world was built for it. To house it, to care for it. What is seen is merely a construct for the eyes to understand, its full majesty is beyond comprehension. It is not just an orb, it is an algorithm that equals so much more.

The women understand this. They understand that much of the universe is illusory. It is pointless and cruel, but that is the joke of cosmic nihilism. Some would seek to impose order, but it is a child's pursuit. And children wearing the flesh of elders are the biggest jokes of all.

Audrey was rocketed back to her place on the bed, her head throbbing.

"What the fuck was that?" asked Roma.

"Huh?" tried Audrey.

"You went all Zen and your skin turned black, like your Crimsonata blood."

"I went to, I don't know, the source? The place my blood comes from and where Crimsonata spirits retire to," she said. "It's hard to explain. I think it tried to tell me something, but I'm not sure."

Roma crossed her arms. "So you have throwing knives, healing powers, and a magic trance. Any other abilities I should know about?"

"Um, not that I know of at the moment. Oh, except this one, which kinda doesn't count."

Audrey formed the ball of blood in her hand and held it there for a moment before absorbing it back in.

"Yeah, that one's kind of lame."

"Agreed," said Audrey.

Roma sighed. "I know I'm supposed to call this in, but I'm going to wait. I need to call in our success on the werewolf hunt anyhow, but we'll do it later tomorrow. How about we explore your powers first?"

Audrey nodded. "That sounds good, I guess. You really think they won't just... you know?"

"They're not going to kill you. Honestly, after everything, they're liable to want to put you in an Adept cell."

"With other magical people?"

"Yeah," said Roma walking away from her.

"You're mad. I'm sorry! I didn't mean for this to happen, really?"

"I'm not mad, Audrey," said Roma. "I like working with you, okay? I don't want to get split up. In case you haven't noticed, I don't have a lot of friends."

"Oh," said Audrey.

"So yeah, BFF's and all that shit. Now let's get some sleep, okay?"

Audrey smiled.

CHAPTER 47

Across the street from the motel was a dive bar called the Country Clink. It was an establishment known for watered down beer, fights in the parking lot, and a honky-tonk jukebox. Most of the patrons were of the good 'ol boy variety, those who drove pickup trucks and spit chewing tobacco. Far from the South here in Utah, a good number of them still thought it was appropriate to have confederate flags emblazoned upon their vehicles or shirts, more for the racist statement than anything else. The few women haunting the bar were seen as little more than decorative ornaments.

Tommy Ray was one of the average patrons of the Country Clink, a regular who showed up most nights to whittle away his meager paycheck on piss warm beer and handfuls of peanuts. He knew no other life and had found a certain contentment in it. But even the Clink had rules, so he had to step outside to smoke. Another way those damn liberals were taking away all his rights. Going to light up, he paused with the lighter half way to his mouth when he saw the... person... step around the corner of the building.

Tommy Ray turned and threw the door open. "Jim Buck, Scully, Deano, everybody get the fuck out here! Now!"

He looked back to the figure crossing the lot and scowled. "Hold it right there, freak!"

The person stopped. Tommy Ray stormed across the gravel lot, hearing the others hoot and holler as they followed behind him. He couldn't believe his eyes.

Was it a chick or a dude? Tommy Ray couldn't tell. It was nearly as tall as him, and Tommy Ray was over six feet. Skinny little shit, what his mom would've called willowy. Wearing some kind of skin-tight white jumpsuit. Bare feet, albino pale. Its white hair looked weird in the night, too. Like milk or some shit. It blinked its beady red eyes at Tommy Ray.

"I search for a woman," it said in a reedy, high-pitched voice.

"Think the only woman here is you," said Scully with a laugh.

"I am a pure being, beyond the need for gender and sex."

Tommy Ray scowled deeper. More hippie-dippie bullshit. He didn't know who this freak was, but they had wandered their skinny ass into the wrong parking lot. A woman should know her place, and a man should be a man. Anything different was wrong and needed that nonsense beaten straight.

"So you ain't a woman then, that what you're saying?" asked Tommy Ray.

"I am non-binary. I am unified unlike you primates. Now, tell me where the woman is."

"The only bitch gonna be here is you," said Tommy Ray, taking a swing.

The slender individual dodged, then stepped out of the way of the second swing. Tommy Ray kept swinging wildly, kept missing. Finally the stranger reached out and grabbed him by the face. He went rigid at the touch.

"You are an animal, a low beast. You grunt and bleat and thrash about. I would see you lower."

Particles of light burst out from the hand gripping Tommy Ray's face and infused his body. Dropping to the ground, he began to shake, his body racked with convulsions. His friends called out to him but were all too cowardly to rush to his aid. Flesh began to burst through his clothing, muscles ripping out upon muscles, bones shattering and reforming in new patterns. Mutating, devolving. Organs slipping out in sacks and lying on the ground, skin folding over their vacancies. Teeth sprouting out in new mouths, salivating, then sealing shut. Vestigial appendages, some without a skeletal structure, wobbling and flailing. The whole bulbous form had doubled Tommy Ray's original size, excreting fluids and emitting hideous wails.

The whole transformation had taken a little over a single minute.

Some of Tommy Ray's friends had fled. Others had stayed, transfixed by terror.

"I search for a woman," said the individual in white. "You may know her as the Crimsonata. You may know her as Audrey Lyn Darrow. She is here, she is near. Bring her to me and I will kill you. I will kill you as opposed to this."

Deano pulled out his piece and shot the stranger three times in the chest.

They watched in horror as the stranger stumbled back, the white hair that wasn't hair, but something liquid, something more like milk, flowed down the body. It filled the holes, healing the wounds. Even the jumpsuit repaired itself.

"I am a superior being," it said. "I am physical matter transcendent. Here on a glorious mission of retribution, your feeble attempts at aggression cannot harm me. You cannot protect her. I will see the Crimsonata erased from this universe."

"We don't know who the fuck you're talking about!" said Scully.

The pale face split into a smile. "I will test the veracity of that."

Particles of light exploded out, showering most of the men. Even those hit with only a few shimmering specks of illumination went down screaming. Their bodies began to turn on them, betray them, churning and shifting. Those who had been mercifully unaffected now ran, and they were allowed. Those less in the grips of the mutagenic properties screamed and begged for death. The white clad individual strode up to the nearest one of them and knelt down.

"The Crimsonata. Small in stature, yellow of hair. Twenty-five of your years. Where is she?"

"Please! Oh god, ahhhhh... no!"

"She may have a man with her, a brother. Tall, brown of hair. Where?"

"The pain, please! It huuurts!"

With a frown, more particles were released onto the man's face, turning it into what looked like a mass of tumors. He was still alive, but silent.

Kneeling down at the next screaming man, the questions began again.

"The Crimsonata, where is she?"

CHAPTER 48

"What the hell was that?" asked Roma.

Audrey was about to get in the shower, but turned around instead, listening. They sounded like screams. Not fun screams but screams of agony.

"Sounds close," said Roma, getting up from the bed and crossing the room to look out of the window. "More than one person, too."

"You don't think we missed a werewolf, do you?"

"I don't know, but we better gear up."

Audrey raced over and pulled her socks and shoes back on. Most of her equipment was still laying in a pile where she had dropped it. She slid the belt back on and buckled it, adjusting the holsters. Two handguns slid into them and she filled the other waiting spaces with easy release extra clips. She slipped on the shoulder harness that housed her shotgun and machete along her back, the shells stored in a string along the left of her torso. Various sized knives went back in place at her wrists, ankles, thighs, and lower back.

Finally, she flexed her fingers and called up the blood. It flowed up from her fingertips and moved in tendrils. In her mind she saw those thin ropes extending, whipping out and severing through flesh. She had her own weapon if she needed it.

Roma finished getting all of her things in order and headed to the door. She paused and grabbed the keys, looking around. The screams had gotten louder.

"Let's go."

Audrey nodded and followed her out.

They stalked across the parking lot, hands on their weapons. The screams were coming from across the street. There was a shithole bar there, one Roma had remarked upon when they pulled in, a place that was the very definition of a redneck hovel. The women moved down along the motel toward it, passing doors.

Roma peeked out from around the corner and scoped out the scene across the street. "People are laying all over the parking lot, naked. I think there's something wrong with them. They look... out of proportion."

"What?"

"Look for yourself."

Audrey peered around the edge of the motel and took in the scene. The people did indeed look wrong, misshaped. Half undressed, too? Easily a dozen of them rolled around in the gravel, wailing. A single person, dressed all in white, strolled among them, saying something she couldn't make out.

"We've got what looks to be one perp in white over there," said Audrey.

"I caught that. Could be anything, too. How do you want to play this?"

Audrey eyed the parking lot from where they were. There was no way to sneak over there, the area wide and open. Darkness wouldn't give them that much cover, especially with the lights from the motel and the bar. Trying to make their way around to the back of the bar would take too long.

"Unfortunately, I'm thinking straight up."

Roma smiled. "My thoughts exactly. I've got the shotgun, you come in with the handguns. Feel free to jump in with your powers if need be."

Audrey nodded and pulled out her Glocks. The women held eyes for a moment and then moved. Not quite running, but moving fast enough, they closed the gap between the motel and the parking lot. As soon as they hit gravel, they were issuing demands.

"Lay down on the ground, on the ground now!"

"Put your hands behind your head!"

"Get down and..."

Both women began to see exactly what had happened to the people flailing and seeping around them, the human monstrosities sculpted out of skin and muscle, bone and fluid. Audrey fought to keep her vomit down as one reached out with something like a flippered hand and patted at her shoe, spitting up pus all over itself. The creatures howled in a cacophony.

"You!" proclaimed the figure in white, a slender finger pointed at Audrey.

"Me?"

"The Adversary, The Nemesis, The Celestial Whore!"

"What the fuck?" asked Roma.

Audrey stared at the androgynous figure and sighed. It was albino skinned, with red eyes, and wore a skintight white jumpsuit. The white outfit would have been enough, but the liquid hair that cascaded over its shoulders like milk gave it away. Something from the Ovessa, something sent back up.

"I was birthed for one glorious reason," it said. "To restore honor to the Ovessa! To slay the Crimsonata who dared turn the Outer Gods against the Most Holy and then subjugate this world in its name. All in the honor of the Ovessa, all in the honor of my maker!"

"Okay," said Roma, who fired the shotgun twice straight into its chest.

The Ovessa's child stumbled back, but the liquid from its hair flowed down and reworked its wounds, sealing them and healing them. Within only seconds, the figure was standing straight again and smiling at them.

"I am a perfect physical being, crafted by the Ovessa as its only true offspring. It's avatar. Every atom of me is me, held together by the inextinguishable light of the Ovessa's realm. I am unified, eternal, and I am going to lay waste to this planet once I show you torment on a cosmic scale."

Particles of light began to dance from its hands as a smile broke wide along its pale face.

Audrey backed up, calling up the blood, ready to act.

Then the night sky broke open.

A solid column of black lightning rocketed down from the heavens and impacted the figure in white directly, obliterating it to nothingness. The air burned with celestial intent, the psychic aftermath like thunder in your skull. Audrey couldn't even move enough to fall, paralyzed by the physical manifestation of divine will.

The dark electricity began to disperse, reform, and crackle into shape. Where the child of the Ovessa once stood, Mr. Inanis now stepped out.

He looked at both women. "So, how have we been?"

CHAPTER 49

A udrey stared at Inanis.

"Not that I'm not thankful for your help, but what the hell?"

"Yeah, that was our fault. The Ovessa found a loophole. It created a true separate entity, one that could move independently beyond its realm. The Ovessite. It was looking for some payback, I guess."

Roma narrowed her eyes. "And you saved us out of the kindness of your heart?"

Inanis laughed. "Oh, of course not. The Ovessa belongs to us and everything it creates is ours. We just wanted to make sure."

"And all these people?" shouted Audrey, gesturing to all the mutated folks lying in the parking lot.

"What about them?" asked Inanis, looking mystified.

Audrey shook her head. Nothing changed. She had joined the Promethean Wall to protect people from Inanis just as much as from things like The Ovessite. Things with too much power and no idea how to wield it over humans.

"Audrey has her powers back," said Roma. "Why is that?"

"How would I know?"

"I thought you said I wouldn't be the Crimsonata anymore. Are the Outer Gods coming back after me?" asked Audrey.

"Did I specifically say that? I don't recall. I guess through millennia of breeding, it's become part of you. Maybe the Ovessite's arrival kick started something. Maybe it was something else."

Audrey peered at him. "How did you know it was recently?"

Inanis smiled. "Oh Audrey, you know you're one of my favorite mortals. I keep an eye on you. Hell, I might have saved you even if it hadn't been in our own interests."

Audrey didn't know how she felt about that. Inanis had orchestrated her entire life, even the killing of her mother. He gave moral relativism a whole new definition. At the same time, having something so unbelievably powerful on your side probably wasn't a bad idea.

"Well, I should go. I get to go down and tell the Ovessa I just killed its kid. That'll be fun. You two don't die now."

And he was gone.

Roma looked at Audrey. "Have you ever stopped and considered what a really weird life we have?"

"Yes. Often."

"We're going to need to drag all these bodies into the bar and set it on fire."

"I'm surprised no one has driven past yet."

"Don't jinx it, Audrey. Don't jinx it."

It took two hours, but they got it done. A bullet to the head of each victim, a blaze that would cover up a lot of the madness. Oh, there would be questions, but the town was too small to afford to look too deeply into it all. The families would not have answers, but it was better that way.

Roma had thought it best if they hacked up the mutated bodies. At first, they used machetes, but then Audrey thought to use her powers. Utilizing the blood, she created long, twisting blades that sliced right through the bodies with ease. All mental and no muscle, it took her twenty minutes to dispatch fourteen bodies. They scattered the pieces around the bar haphazardly.

It was nearing dawn by the time the two women made their way back to the motel. Audrey was exhausted and felt disgusting. At the same time, she felt like she had truly finished a chapter in her life. The woman from two years ago wouldn't have been able to do the things she had done today. Killed werewolves, faced down an extra-dimensional monster, chopped up dead bodies, and hung out with a god. She'd become someone strong, someone she was proud of being.

She was still that short, weird blonde girl from Cali who liked sci-fi and comics, but now she got to be the heroine. Now she got to make a difference and protect people. That mattered to her.

Roma let her shower first, so she went and stripped down in the bathroom. She stared at her face in the mirror, noticing that she had got some blood in her blonde locks. Once that would've bothered her, now it was just an occupational hazard.

She stepped into the shower, the water hot and steaming. Hopefully the Wall would still want her now that she had her powers, but even if they didn't, Audrey decided she would keep helping people in some way no matter what. She'd figure out a way. It had taken her twenty-five years, but she'd found her path.

It was about choice.

She had chosen to take control of her existence instead of just letting life happen to her. Instead of just being a participant, a passenger. You always have choices, regardless of how distasteful your options are, and those choices can lead to better things. Change can be frightening, but stagnation is deadly. She'd learned that firsthand.

She'd made a lot of choices, a lot of changes. More were coming. But while she was still Audrey, she was a better Audrey. She would handle whatever came. She would have to.

She was the Crimsonata.

EPILOGUE

THREE MONTHS LATER

Audrey Darrow stood before the Council and nodded. The Promethean Wall had been surprised to learn that she had regained her abilities as The Crimsonata but were not immediately dismissive. After displaying her powers to them through a series of tests, they had become more accepting. Over the last few months, Audrey had grown proficient in over a dozen different ways to manipulate the blood, both offensively and defensively, as well as ways more esoteric. The Council marveled at the versatility of her abilities and the control she had over them. She did her best to explain the connection she had with her lineage and how that informed her skills.

She also explained that the Crimsonata had always been a protector, a leader, a healer. She felt it was in her best interest, as the latest incarnation of the Crimsonata, to be with the Wall, that she could do the most good with them.

Audrey liked to think her little speech was what sold them.

Now she was being told that she was going to be assembled into a new Adept cell, something the Council had been wanting to put together for a year. Allison Roma would be joining since she had proved herself in the field and had the specific background they were looking for. Her sister had died under the machinations of a spell caster, making her wary of magic – which was why she was being entrusted with an e-grimoire containing over one thousand arcane texts. She wasn't terribly pleased about the assignment, but knew she was suited for the position.

A third member of the cell would be reporting to them when they got to Cleveland. Audrey didn't know much about him, only that he was psychically gifted. Telepathy, psychometry, some minor telekinesis. That could come in handy.

"Do you have any other questions, Ms. Darrow?" asked one of the Council members.

"Yes," said Audrey. "When do we begin?"

END

ABOUT THE AUTHOR

Brian Fatah Steele has been writing various types of dark fiction for over ten years, from horror to urban fantasy and science fiction. Growing up hooked on comic books and monster movies, his work gravitates towards anything imaginative and dynamic. Steele originally went to school for fine arts but finds himself far more fulfilled now by storytelling.

His work has appeared in such places as 4POCALYPSE, BLOOD TYPE, CTHULHU LIES DREAMING, 4RCHETYPES, DEATH'S REALM, THE IDOLATERS OF CTHULHU, PAYING THE FERRYMAN, and the Bram Stoker Award-nominated DARK VISIONS, VOL.1. His own titles include the sci-fi horror novel THERE IS DARKNESS IN EVERY ROOM, the urban fantasy novel IN BLEED COUNTRY, the post-mythic novella collection FURTHER THAN FATE, and the dark sci-fi collection BRUTAL STARLIGHT.

Steele lives in Ohio with a few cats and survives on a diet of coffee and cigarettes. He spends his time still dabbling in visual art, vowing to fix up his house, acting as a part-time chaos entity, spending too many hours watching television, and probably working on his next writing project.

https://www.amazon.com/Brian-Fatah-Steele/e/B002V7OJR0/

https://twitter.com/brian_f_steele

https://www.facebook.com/brianfatahsteele

**FINALLY IN PRINT AFTER MORE THAN THREE DECADES,
THE NOVEL MARK MORRIS WROTE <u>BEFORE</u> *TOADY***

EVIL NEEDS ONLY A SEED

Limefield has had more than its fair share of tragedy. Barely six years ago, a disturbed young boy named Russell Swaney died beneath the wheels of a passenger train mere moments after committing a heinous act of unthinkable sadism. Now, a forest fire caused by the thoughtless actions of two teens has laid waste to hundreds of acres of the surrounding woodlands and unleashed a demonic entity

EVIL TAKES ROOT

Now, a series of murders plague the area and numerous local residents have been reported missing, including the entire population of the nearby prison. But none of this compares to the appearance of the Winter Tree, a twisted wooden spire which seems to leech the warmth from the surrounding land.

EVIL FLOURISHES

Horrified by what they have caused, the two young men team up with a former teacher and the local police constabulary to find the killer, but it may already be too late. Once planted, evil is voracious. Like a weed, it strangles all life, and the roots of the Winter Tree are already around their necks.

Available in paperback or Kindle on Amazon.com

http://bit.ly/TreeKindle

There's a monster coming to the small town of Pikeburn. In half an hour, it will begin feeding on the citizens, but no one will call the authorities for help. They are the ones who sent it to Pikeburn. They are the ones who are broadcasting the massacre live to the world. Every year, Red Diamond unleashes a new creation in a different town as a display of savage terror that is part warning and part celebration. Only no one is celebrating in Pikeburn now. No one feels honored or patriotic. They feel like prey.

Local Sheriff Yan Corban refuses to succumb to the fear, paranoia, and violence that suddenly grips his town. Stepping forward to battle this year's lab-grown monster, Sheriff Corban must organize a defense against the impossible. His allies include an old art teacher, a shell-shocked mechanic, a hateful millionaire, a fearless sharpshooter, a local meth kingpin, and a monster groupie. Old grudges, distrust, and terror will be the monster's allies in a game of wits and savagery, ambushes and treachery. As the conflict escalates and the bodies pile up, it becomes clear this creature is unlike anything Red Diamond has unleashed before.

No mercy will be asked for or given in this battle of man vs monster. It's time to run, hide, or fight. It's time for Red Diamond.

Available in paperback or Kindle on Amazon.com

http://bit.ly/DiamondUS

January 12, 1888

When a day dawns warm and mild in the middle of a long cold winter, it's greeted as a blessing, a reprieve. A chance for those who've been cooped up indoors to get out, do chores, run errands, send the children to school... little knowing that they're only seeing the calm before the storm.

The blizzard hits out of nowhere, screaming across the Great Plains like a runaway train. It brings slicing winds, blinding snow, plummeting temperatures. Livestock will be found frozen in the fields, their heads encased in blocks of ice formed from their own steaming breath. Frostbite and hypothermia wait for anyone caught without shelter.

For the hardy settlers of Far Enough, in the Montana Territory, it's about to get worse. Something else has arrived with the blizzard. Something sleek and savage and hungry. Wild animal or vengeful spirit from native legend, it blends into the snow and bites with sharper teeth than the wind.

It is called the *wanageeska*.

It is the White Death

ON THE HORIZON FROM
BLOODSHOT BOOKS
2019-20*

The Devil Virus – Chris DiLeo

What Sleeps Beneath – John Quick

The Cryptids – Elana Gomel

Dead Sea Chronicles – Tim Curran

Midnight Solitaire – Greg F. Gifune

Dead Branches – Benjamin Langley

The October Boys – Adam Millard

Clownflesh – Tim Curran

Blood Mother: A Novel of Terror – Pete Kahle

Not Your Average Monster – World Tour

The Abomination (The Riders Saga #2) – Pete Kahle

The Horsemen (The Riders Saga #3) – Pete Kahle

other titles to be added when confirmed

BLOODSHOT BOOKS

READ UNTIL YOU BLEED!

CPSIA information can be obtained
at www.ICGtesting.com
Printed in the USA
LVHW041811230623
750626LV00001B/163